P9-EFI-927

Secrets of a Housewife

Secrets of a Housewife

J. Tremble

Kensington Publishing Corp.
http://www.kensingtonbooks.com

DAFINA BOOKS are published by

Kensington Publishing Corp.
119 West 40th Street
New York, NY 10018

Copyright © 2006 by J. Tremble

All rights reserved. No part of this book may be repro-
duced in any form or by any means without the prior written consent of the Publisher, excepting brief quotes used
in reviews.

If you purchased this book without a cover, you should be
aware that this book is stolen property. It was reported as
"unsold and destroyed" to the Publisher and neither the
Author nor the Publisher has received any payment for
this "stripped book."

All Kensington Titles, Imprints, and Distributed Lines are
available at special quantity discounts for bulk purchases
for sales promotions, premiums, fund-raising, and educa-
tional or institutional use. Special book excerpts or cus-
tomized printings can also be created to fit specific needs.
For details, write or phone the office of the Kensington
special sales manager: Kensington Publishing Corp., 119
West 40th Street, New York, NY 10018, attn: Special Sales
Department, Phone: 1-800-221-2647.

Dafina and the Dafina logo Reg. U.S. Pat. & TM Off.

ISBN-13: 978-0-7582-6323-0
ISBN-10: 0-7582-6323-6

First Kensington mass market printing: September 2011

10 9 8 7 6 5 4 3 2 1

Printed in the United States of America

*I would like to dedicate this first novel to my
wonderful mother, beautiful wife,
and caring children.*

*In loving memory of my sister,
Lena Victoria Johnson-Griffin*

I Love You All!

Chapter 1

Just like any other Tuesday evening, Tarron watched his son Terrance at football practice. Tarron's hard, sculpted body was pressed against the south side goalpost when his phone rang. He knew the number very well. It was the number of the pay phone that his wife normally called from on her nights to pick up Terrance from practice.

Tarron wondered how his wife could be on the field and not come over and speak to him face-to-face. He also wondered why she'd be at practice on his night.

"Hey, baby," he said as he answered the phone.

"This isn't your baby, but your Peekaboo," the seductive voice replied. "I know I shouldn't be here, but I couldn't resist. How about you walk

into the wooded path behind the pay phones
and come warm my buns?"

Tarron felt his heart drop into his stomach.
He began to look around, to his right, then to
his left. His pulse raced out of control. This
excitement made his dick hard. He pressed
END on his phone and jetted toward his desti-
nation. The bulge in his pants screamed to
make it to the end of the wooded path. With
every step he took, small beads of sweat
formed on his cheeks.

He was halfway up the path when he felt a
hand pull him into a covered patch. Before
he could speak, Victoria grabbed his curly
locks and began to kiss him softly on the lips.
The kissing got hotter as he slowly slid his
frozen fingertips down her back. Victoria felt
chills glide down her spine. Instantly, Tarron
became aware of the nakedness underneath
her black miniskirt. "Oh hell," he cheered.

Despite the cold November breeze, their
excitement for one another caused sweat to
drench their foreheads. His zipper slid open
as he rubbed his pelvic area firmly against
hers. There was extreme passion in the way he
kissed her. Nothing like the friendly kisses he
gave Secret. It was as if he had walked for days
in the burning hot sun in an African desert
and her lips were the water he desperately
needed to survive.

Suddenly, Victoria broke away from Tarron's kiss. Extremely flexible, she raised her right leg above her shoulder. Tarron bent to his knees and used his tongue to moisten her treasure. The thickness of his tongue caressed her favorite G-spot. Victoria began to bite her upper lip as the pleasure increased. Tarron grabbed hold of her butt as he buried his entire face into her flowing juices. Victoria squeezed his head tightly. She wanted to take all of him, but his tongue was too tantalizing.

A whistle sounded from a distance, which made it clear that practice was still in session. Distracted by the yelling coach, Victoria lost hold of her leg, and it came crashing down on Tarron's head. He rose out of anxiety from the pain, staring straight into her eyes.

In one quick movement, his pants were open, and he pressed his hard shaft firmly inside her. Backing her into a tree, Tarron began pounding. Her juices streamed as he played tag with her erogenous zones. Victoria's slight cry confirmed that she was indeed being taken care of.

In and out he moved. Up and down she moved in response. Grabbing the back of his neck, she dug her nails into his mocha skin. The sharp pain forced his rod to stretch and fill her completely. Tarron's teeth sank into

Victoria's shoulder. Reaching his climax, he trembled like a helpless dog.

Tarron wanted to yell out in pleasure, but this was not the ideal place to draw attention to himself. He buried his face in her breast and let out a silent moan. Victoria bent over to kiss the top of his head, still desiring more. Seconds passed and Victoria began to grip his shaft with intense force. The glaze in her eyes warned Tarron that it wasn't over.

He worked hard to get back to full length. Victoria pushed him back when she felt his penis inflate. Victoria turned around and bent over, pressing her hands against the tree. He lifted her tiny skirt and slowly slid his penis through the shaking walls of her vagina once again. Tarron tapped her spot at different speeds until the words struggled to flow from her lips.

"I'm cumming. . . . Don't stop," Victoria begged.

Just then the whistle blew again. Practice was over. Quickly, the children's voices seemed to grow closer. Still caught by passion, Tarron lay comfortably inside her sugar walls.

"Someone's coming," she said. Tarron pulled back his thickness, and they snickered as they rushed to fix their clothes. They moved like naughty high school kids making out behind the bleachers.

Victoria was the first to appear from behind the bushes. As Tarron followed, he noticed his son taking a leak next to a nearby tree. Panicking, he stopped in his tracks. His first reaction was to back up toward the woods. But before he knew it, he and Terrance had made eye contact. Tarron wondered how much his son had heard. Terrance froze. He noticed his father and a strange woman standing close together. He stared at Victoria with extreme hatred, and then his little head twisted back and forth, from Victoria to his dad.

"Boy, you scared the shit out of me," Tarron yelled, jarring Terrance from his trance.

Terrance ignored his father's words. Tarron knew there would be trouble in paradise. He could read Terrance's mind. *Ooh, I'm going to tell Momma. Make me mad.* Tarron felt controlled by his eight-year-old son—not a good position for a father to be in.

Speechless, Terrance quickly shook himself a couple of times and darted back to the field. Victoria vanished into thin air.

During the car ride home, Tarron contemplated a discussion with Terrance about the woods scene but decided against it. The thick silence in the air made the ride seem even longer than usual.

As they pulled up the long brick driveway, Secret was sweeping the leaves off the porch.

"How was practice, sweetie?" she asked as Terrance shut the car door.

Once again Tarron's pulse rate increased as Terrance looked back at him. He was still dazed and took a long pause before answering his mother. All Tarron could think about was Terrance exposing his dirty little *secret.*

Terrance looked back at his mother and said, "It was okay." Then he darted into the house to change his clothes.

As Tarron walked up the driveway, the vibration on his hip startled him. He looked down at the screen of his cell phone and recognized the code. Meaningless to others, the message definitely meant everything to him. It was from Victoria. Each number represented a letter, and decoded, it read: You are the best thing that ever happened to me.

"Look, Daddy, I can ride my bike by myself," his daughter said, breaking his trance. Her lips trembled from the cold air.

"I'm so proud of you, baby," he replied.

He stood on the porch and watched his little angel ride up and down the sidewalk. Without notice his wife took position next to him. "Our little girl sure is growing up," she said as she slipped her arms around Tarron's

6

waist. Secret watched Tarron like a love-struck newlywed.

"It was just yesterday when she learned how to walk," he added. Tarron met Secret's stare momentarily.

"I made your favorite dish. The rice will be ready in ten minutes. Besides, the temperature is dropping. Bring the children in soon and wash up for dinner."

Tarron was bored with the routine of marriage. Each day had become a bore. First small talk with the wife, then playtime with the children, then family dinner discussion about everyone's day, homework, and the list went on.

As for sex with his wife, he could set his calendar by it. It happened every Wednesday night, just before the second episode of *Law & Order*, or occasionally when she was feeling frisky. She claimed to always be tired from keeping house. But when it did occur, it lacked excitement. Lying in the bed, Secret gave him the signal by rolling close to him. She threw her leg up across him. At that moment, Tarron rolled on his back. The two exchanged a couple of slight pecks and removed their pj's. A few strokes from him, a short heaving moan from her, and seconds later the snoring contest began.

Their sex life was nothing compared to the one he had with Victoria. As Tarron made himself comfortable on the porch, he thought back to one episode in particular. One rainy night, as planned, Tarron paid Victoria a late-night visit. Instead of knocking on her front door, he entered through the back bedroom window. He tapped on it because he knew she was up and waiting. When she lifted the blind, he got hotter seeing what she wore.

He climbed through the window, stripping off every piece of clothing. It was about business. They went straight to the grind. After hours of hot, passionate sex, their special scent filled the space. They each took on each other's bodily fragrance. Drenched in sweat, he caught a glimpse of her eyes from the moonlight shining through the skylight and fell in love with her all over again.

Suddenly his suspicions were raised by another tap on the window. He instantly thought that his woman was seeing another man. Calmly, Victoria lifted the blinds, and to Tarron's surprise, a tall, slender woman stood waiting to enter. His rage quickly turned to shock. No words were spoken. The woman climbed into the room and dropped her raincoat. Naked, Victoria smiled and invited her to come and join in on the fun.

"Move over," she said as she guided Victoria aside.

She straddled Tarron like a nasty stripper giving her client a seductive lap dance. Tarron looked at Victoria, and in her eyes there was no hint of surprise. He had died and gone to heaven. It was events like this that kept Tarron from being faithful. Who could choose tradition over way-out, extravagant episodes like that?

Life wasn't always dull with Secret, he thought. When they first started dating, their relationship resembled one of a fairy tale. They would talk on the phone until they both fell asleep, and always picked the wildest places to make love.

Tarron recalled once how Secret truly showed off her talents. After a movie, they had dinner at a jazz restaurant. On their way home, Secret turned into the driveway of a local high school that was closed for renovation.

She parked the car and told Tarron to grab the basket in the trunk and follow her. Of course, he followed her. She moved down the walkway, through the gates to the football field, down the stands, and to the north side end zone.

She took out a blindfold and covered his

eyes. "Trust me, baby," she whispered in his ear as she concealed his eyes.

As Tarron stood there in complete darkness, the sounds of the world became amplified. The roaring of the engines of passing cars vibrated his body. Goose bumps rose on Tarron's arms when neighborhood dogs began barking. He could hear Secret unzipping her pants and unsnapping the buttons to her blouse. Tarron wondered what Secret had pulled out of the basket after hearing it close. Her footsteps grew closer.

She told him to remove the blindfold. There she was, lying under a white blanket on top of a blue comforter. "Come show me some of those tackling moves you brag about. Give me a touchdown," she said as she lifted the blanket to show off her naked body.

She watched as his left hand moved up to the zipper of his sweat jacket. Her lips moistened as he opened his jacket. He tossed it upon the basket and continued with his T-shirt. The brisk wind blew across his bare chest. Tarron's cut body made up for his average looks. Jokingly, he rolled his shirt into a ball and threw it at Secret.

She raised her arm, still clinging to the blanket, forming a shield to block the oncoming object. Pulling on the blanket, he uncovered the flower tattoo drawn over her left ankle. He paused long enough to notice each stroke of the artistic creation. Dropping down to his right knee, he licked both petals. His tongue followed the outline of her flower, leading him to her calf. He began to massage her calf, her thigh, and then her hips.

Secret became aggressive. Pulling Tarron onto his back, she began to untie the strings to his sweatpants. Tiny kisses flooded his chest. Her thick tongue swirled inside his navel. He felt her hardened nipples sliding down his pelvic area.

Tarron jerked. Secret's hands were cold to the touch as she caressed his manhood. Sounds of the night collaborated to produce a symphonic harmony. This rhythm brought warmth to him. Secret wanted to feel Tarron inside of her. She straddled him and inserted his penis in her awaiting vagina. Using the sounds of the night, she ground her hips to the inner-city beats. Tarron partook in the erotic dance. He used the old-school blue-light house party movements to respond to each of Secret's grinds.

Secret arched her back to grind even harder. This was a movement she knew that Tarron loved. Controlled by his passion, he pulled on the blanket and curled his toes. Secret watched as his tongue began to lick his lips in a circular motion. Whenever she would grind real hard, his tongue would pause at the center of his upper lip. Secret started raising and lowering her wet vagina, allowing his penis to almost exit her, then fully enter again. She enjoyed squeezing him as she lowered her body back down. The walls of her vagina were so soft and wet that it had Tarron on the verge of orgasmic gratification.

Tarron rolled Secret over onto her back without allowing his penis to leave Secret's garden. Even though it felt good having Secret on top, Tarron knew that she liked having him on top the most. He raised her legs toward the sky and began moving in and out with slow full-body jerks.

Tarron lifted his upper body into the air with his arms and started moving faster and faster inside her. Secret's body shook with delight. Tarron reached another climax, but this time he was not alone. Both of them came with so much force that their bodies went limp.

They lay with their bodies connected like jigsaw puzzle pieces. Not even the wino using the field as a shortcut was able to interrupt this portrait of intimacy. Tarron believed that this type of lovemaking would be enough to make their marriage last . . . last forever. Secret showed him differently.

The tapping of small hands brought Tarron back to the present. He grabbed his daughter by the hand in pursuit of fulfilling his fatherly duties. Tired from his foul play at the field, Tarron rushed to unwind for the evening.

That night, as he and Secret rested in their bed, laughing at a scene on the sitcom *Martin*, they were interrupted by a knock at the door.

"Come in. It's open," Tarron yelled.

Terrance pushed open the door, came in halfway, and stood right in front of the television. "I just wanted to say good night."

"Ah, you are such a sweet child," Secret said.

Terrance gave her a big hug and even bigger smile. He then turned to Tarron and said, "Practice sure was good today, huh, Dad?"

"You looked pretty good out there, but you still need to hit a little harder."

"I need to stick it to 'em hard like you. I mean like you used to do, huh?"

Tarron sat up in the bed and gave Terrance a cold look. His expression read, *Start some shit and see where you end up.* Terrance quickly turned and ran out of the room.

Secret rolled over. She was dumbfounded. "What do you think that was all about?"

13

Tarron clicked the power button on the remote and shrugged his shoulders. He turned his back toward Secret and stared out the bedroom window.

Chapter 2

Tarron was standing in the warm water in the Cayman Islands to catch his breath when suddenly he felt soft hands caress his legs from underneath. The hands traveled with a purpose, stroking his manhood. Tarron's breathing intensified.

"Honey, it's my sister and her family. Come down and say hello," Secret shouted, breaking his fantasy.

"I'm coming now," he said dryly. *I wish I was cumming*, he thought jokingly to himself.

Frustrated, Tarron got up from the bed and headed for the bathroom to freshen his breath.

As he faced the mirror, he found himself sinking back into the previous, seductive images in his mind. He realized the hands were those of

Victoria, the woman who gave him reason to live. In seconds, he felt movement inside his trunks. He fell back against the shower door; his heart rate tripled. This time she stopped at his waist. He could feel the heat from her body. She leaned in against him.

Tarron slowly leaned forward, as if she were really there, and started to move his lips in a circular motion. Victoria maneuvered her tongue in a twirling motion inside his mouth. So he thought. For Tarron, this was heaven, so he opted to take it slow. He embraced the air, as if to hold her tight, with his hands on her lower back.

"I feel your hardness," he heard Victoria whisper. Unable to handle his own passion, he helplessly grabbed the baby oil from the vanity. He dripped it slowly over his shaft. Stroking it, he grew weak at the knees. Tarron forgot where he was. The hardness of his penis sliding against her inner thigh caused him to lose sight of Victoria altogether. He became a one-man show. Gentle, then rapid movements of his hand sent him soaring from the ground. He had yearned for Victoria daily and wanted to savor that moment.

Tarron found himself strung out on the floor. Startled by a noise from the door, he jumped. He looked up in shame. How would he explain the towel draped across his penis to Secret? Relieved, he shoved Fluffy, the family cat, through the cracked door. He pulled himself together and headed downstairs. Damn that was good.

Tarron loved his wife with all his heart and wanted to work at renewing the spark in their marriage. He believed Secret possessed all the qualities a wife should. She cooked, cleaned, spent quality time with the children, and loved everything about him. She loved the way he smelled, the way he smiled. Correction, *the way he used to smile.* Still, Tarron couldn't forget that just because Secret was next to perfect didn't change the fact that he was no longer happy. Besides, Victoria was an addiction. He was a pipe head for her love, and she was the crack he needed to function.

As he took the first step down the stairs, he dreaded the hours of agony ahead. He had to deal with Secret's sister Doris, Motherdear, and his brother, Jay—the entire Thanksgiving Day. Doris was one of those women who believed everything had to be perfect. She wanted to live like the Cosbys, but reality taught her differently. Though she had a graduate degree in psychology, she stayed broke trying to keep up with the Joneses. She and her husband, Stephen, had a big house they couldn't afford. But Tarron figured that was what he got for not manning up. As for his mother and brother, together, they always brought the drama. He gathered his senses before he reached the last step and greeted their guests.

"Doris, Stephen, good to see you," he said.

"Tarron." Stephen smiled.

"Hi, Tee. How you been?" Doris asked, looking him up and down.

Tarron gave Doris a meaningless hug, almost snagging her weave. He shook Stephen's hand as he let her go.

"Where are the kids?" Tarron asked.

"They're running around here somewhere with their cousins." Stephen chuckled.

Secret made room in the coat closet while Stephen and Tarron chatted. Then Secret and Doris went straight into the kitchen to finish dinner. The men hurried into the family room to watch the opening kickoff of the Washington Redskins vs. the Dallas Cowboys football game.

"So, Tarron, how's work?"

"Why? Did Secret tell you something?"

"Naw, Secret didn't tell me nothing," Stephen replied with a strange look. "Was she supposed to?"

"My bad, Steve. You know work is just stressful." Tarron focused his attention on the commercial.

Just then the doorbell rang. Relieved, Tarron excused himself. He peeked through the peephole to see Motherdear and Jay standing on the outside of the door. He yanked it open with a quick motion and screamed, "Let me see some ID."

"Boy, if you don't get out my way, they gon' be tryin' to identify you," replied Motherdear as she pushed her way past Tarron. Motherdear was a large-stature woman, which made her force strong. Tarron flew into the door frame.

"Dumb ass," Jay commented as he passed his brother.

"Don't worry, brother. I've already checked in with your probation officer. I promised him I'd have you home by ten." Tarron felt forced to come up with a comeback for his brother's smart remark.

The room went silent, with the exception of the Pepsi commercial blasting from the television. Everyone knew of the underlying hate they had for each other, but they had never expected Tarron to say something like that. Then suddenly, the uneasiness was broken by three small tornadoes. The amount of noise that came rolling around the corner was a sure sign that Motherdear was in the house. *What would they do without her?* Tarron thought.

"Grandma Motherdear!" the grandchildren screamed.

"Wow, look at my grandbabies. Yaw gettin'

so big." She fixed her eyes on them like they were her prized possessions.

"They should be big. They are always eating. We are going to be in the poorhouse if they keep it up." Stephen laughed. Tarron joined in.

Motherdear shot Stephen a death-defying look. "Aw, shut the hell up." She turned her attention back to the kids. "Yaw must be old as Motherdear now."

The children laughed.

"Come on over here and give me some Motherdear sugar!" She squeezed the children so hard, they could hardly breathe. Her arms were large enough for all five of them— Tarron's two and Doris's three—to fit. Their faces were smashed right in between her big bosoms.

As Tarron sat back and thought about how Motherdear hadn't changed since he was a small boy, on cue Doris stuck her head around the wall and shouted, "Dinner's ready."

"It can't be ready, because I have my cakes and pies in the car." Motherdear pointed her finger at Tarron. "You and your brother, go out and get my bags out the trunk."

They pushed and hit one another as they did what Motherdear told them to do. The table was filled with all the traditional favorites: mouthwatering potato salad, collard greens, mashed potatoes, glazed yams, ham, turkey, and more. Tarron placed the cakes and pies on a separate table off in the corner.

Tarron shouted for Terrance and Tika to get their butts downstairs for dinner. The two children immediately came running, with Lisa, Leslie, and Sean slowly lagging behind.

"Hi, Grandma Motherdear and Uncle Jay," Terrance and Tika shouted.

"Hey, big head. You're starting to look just like your ugly daddy." Jay nudged Terrance in his dome. Tarron rolled his eyes. Secret smiled.

"Get over here and give me some sugar," Motherdear yelled.

As the family gathered around the dinner table, Secret spoke. "Like always, let's bow our heads and thank God for this blessing." After the prayer, each family member had to share what they were thankful for. Tarron hated this custom. Truly, the only thing that could make him happy was being with Victoria. "Let's all say what we are thankful for on this day." Secret was excited.

Tarron breathed heavily. He grinned when his wife looked his way. Secret quickly moved closer to her man and grabbed his hand. Jay quickly made a swinging whip motion with one hand and laughed silently into his other. Tarron gave him a sharp look, then smiled back at Secret.

"I'll start," Doris chimed in. "I'm thankful for my family, all my loved ones having their health, and everyone arriving here safely to share the holiday together."

While each person said what they were thankful for, Tarron held his wife's hand tightly, spacing out several times. He didn't pay full attention until he heard Secret say, "I'm especially thankful for my wonderful husband, who has loved me dearly and stood by my side for the last eight."

"Ahh, that's so . . . sweet," Doris said.

By now, all faces were focused on Tarron, especially Jay's, each person waiting to hear what he'd say. "I'm thankful for all of you," he said, ending with a slight grin. "Especially my wife. Now let's eat."

"That's all you got to say, Mr. Long-Winded?" Jay asked.

"Shut up and sit down, you lonely convict. Maybe if you had a real woman you would understand that they know everything about how you feel by your actions, not your words."

"You both better calm your butts down. I'm not having this mess tonight . . . not this Thanksgiving Day," Motherdear shouted. "Yaw go through this shit every year."

The children all looked at each other, smiled, and began to giggle.

"Excuse me, babies," Motherdear said softly.

As everyone settled down and passed the serving trays around the table, Tarron's face showed no emotion. Secret knew something was going on, as did the others at the dinner table. Everyone decided to leave it alone . . . . all except Doris.

"Tarron, you got something on your mind?" Doris asked.

Yeah, I'd rather be divin' deep into Victoria than into this turkey, he thought, feeling himself growing behind his zipper. *Being around you no-good people, I'm bound to lose my damn mind.*

"Why?" he asked.

Stephen looked up at Tarron, then turned to Doris. "Stop trying to play therapist."

"I'm not," she replied.

"Ever since she went back to school to get her head doctor degree, she has tried to get inside everybody's mind." He looked at her with frustration.

"Whatever!" Doris said with a little head twist. "Pass me the potatoes. You just mad 'cause you didn't finish school."

Every adult braced himself for the drama. Surprisingly, Stephen remained silent. He was more embarrassed than anything.

"I'm sorry. I just got a lot on my mind with work and stuff." Tarron bit into his ham.

"Tarron was promoted to senior partner at the investment firm," Secret added to support her man.

"Congratulations," Doris and Stephen said simultaneously.

"Yeah! Now he's the second man in charge!" Secret grinned proudly.

"Who's the first?" Doris asked sarcastically. "Or should I say CEO?"

"David Jordan," Tarron interjected. "But he's rarely in the office. I'm the main guy for the most part."

"Good for you, son," said Motherdear.

Secret rubbed Tarron's back as she leaned to whisper in his ear. Jay said nothing. He went to reach for another roll from the bread-basket, but it was too far. Secret saw that Jay was having trouble and decided to divert her attention to Jay. As she passed him the bread, their hands accidentally touched.

"Excuse me," Jay said.

Secret lowered her eyes, saying nothing.

"Hey, keep your hands off my woman," Tarron sneered.

"Aw, man, whatever. I got plenty where that came from."

Secret excused herself from the table, returning with desserts in both hands. As she

began to show off her famous German chocolate cake, Tarron could hear the second half
of the football game getting ready to start.

"Honey, I'll take my cake and ice cream in
the family room."

"Me too," Stephen and Jay yelled.

"I cannot believe we are down by ten,"
Tarron cried.

"That's what happens when you like a sorry
team like the Cowgirls. Come over to Redskins land and you'll be a happier man." Jay
turned to Stephen, looking for a supportive
laugh.

"Why are you here *lone star* this year, Jay?"
Stephen wanted no parts of their family feud.
"I look forward to seeing one of those young
beauty queens you usually have on your arm."

"Well, you know, all hos need a break. Pimp
Daddy needed to rest," he replied. Jay lit his
cigarette and smiled.

"In other words, the high schools were
closed, and he couldn't find a date." Tarron
was sick of his brother still trying to be a
mack.

Stephen burst out laughing.

"Man, you're a real ass, you know that?" Jay
said, taking a puff.

"I take after your mother." Tarron waited
for Jay's comeback.

"Hey, Mom, Tarron in here talking about you an ass," Jay shouted.

"If I come in there, I'm gonna whip both his ass and your ass," Motherdear shouted back.

Secret and Doris entered the family room, carrying plates with big slices of chocolate cake and two scoops of vanilla ice cream. Tarron was so heated by his brother's need to be a jerk that he didn't even notice that Doris had handed him his plate. Secret gave the plate she held to Jay. He held on to the plate a little longer than she'd expected. Her look read: *Will you let me let go?* Doris turned and went back into the kitchen.

A commercial showing a picture of the tropics flashed across the TV screen and triggered visions of one of Tarron's episodes with Victoria from earlier that year. Tarron felt himself heating up and quickly excused himself from the room.

"Oh, I forgot that I have to e-mail some information to my project manager for the weekend meeting," he said as he stumbled from his chair.

Secret gave Tarron a quick frown and headed back to the dining room. Tarron wasn't fazed. At that point, his only concern was getting a fix. The basement couldn't be farther away. He pushed the door in a frenzy and flew downstairs to his office. He immediately shut the door behind him. He purposely sat in the dark. Before he could stroke one button on his keyboard, he began to stroke something else. Tarron plopped his head down on the desk and shut his eyes. Instantly, visions of what Victoria did best came to mind. He reflected on one of the better times their lovemaking sent him over the edge. It happened on one of their many getaways. They were fucking on the twenty-sixth-floor balcony of an exquisite hotel in Negril, Jamaica. He recalled licking Victoria's upper body like a lollipop, which turned her on so much that without hesitation, she ripped off her bottoms in a fury.

Tarron tossed her headfirst over the railing. He pulled his erect shaft out of his swimming trunks and lifted Victoria into the air. She felt the night island breeze sweep across her naked butt. She panted before he could put it in.

Tarron gently released his zipper and began another self-pleasuring session with himself. Using his left hand, Tarron inserted every inch of his manhood inside of Victoria. As he stroked himself beneath his desk, he silently gave thanks for the sensational feeling she gave him.

As he hammered in his mind, he whimpered behind closed doors. Hoping no one would enter, he rushed to climax. Tarron visualized Victoria stretching her leg and wrapping it around his back. Forcefully, she began to pound and grind her pelvis. Although Tarron used his muscular, chiseled arms to raise and lower her body, that day he was no match for Victoria. She moaned louder and louder as he deepened his penetration. He could feel the surge of his excretions coming to the head.

Holding her thighs firmly in his hands, he began a reggae popping motion, causing the cum to splash between their bodies—literally. Seconds later, he came back to reality when he felt his stickiness spread all over his hands. Wiping the saliva from his mouth, he licked his own fluids. "Aw shit, this shit is nasty." He jumped up and ran to the bathroom that had recently been added to their basement. He washed both his hands and gargled with Scope. *Now I can e-mail her.*

Victoria,

Another holiday has come, and it hurts me that we are unable to share this day together. I picture you, instead of my wife, conducting the motherly duties of cooking, hosting, and cleaning. Every person around you expecting you to work yourself to the bone because they feel that's your only purpose in this world.

Rest assured, I would feel the complete opposite. In my world, you are a goddess that deserves all the attention. This Thanksgiving Day should consist of everyone around you giving their thanks to you for being so sexy. I'd kill to be with you tonight. We should be together on this day—holding hands or playing a game to see who gives the best head.

Duty Calls,
Love Only Me

He was softly running his fingers across the message written on the computer when he heard a sound behind him. He looked back, and the office door was open slightly. He quickly turned back to his computer screen and clicked the send button. Tarron slowly walked back to the family room, just in time to catch the tail end of the game. The football game ended with Dallas losing to Washington on a last-second field goal attempt. This was clearly not Tarron's night, but at least the Thanksgiving dinner had come to an end.

He and Secret stood on the porch, watching Motherdear and Jay get into their car. They waved at Stephen and Doris as they drove off. Somewhat relieved, Tarron sighed, trying to think of one reason why he'd gotten married. He felt like a prisoner in his own domain. *Married to the wrong woman.*

Tarron stepped back inside and walked toward the kitchen, noticing that every room he passed was immaculate. Even with two children, Secret made sure that everything in the house stayed squeaky clean. Tarron paused by their wedding portrait over the fireplace in the family room. He couldn't help but be proud of the faces that lined the wall. In the picture, it amazed him how much Terrance resembled Secret and Tika resembled him.

He stood behind his wife, Secret, who was extremely shapely despite having had two children. Tarron liked how happy he appeared in the photo. Tika sat in Secret's lap as Terrance leaned on her right shoulder, all three with huge smiles. Tika's missing two front teeth caused Tarron to chuckle. The children were definitely loved.

He wondered momentarily where the spark went. Could he fall in love with her again? To many outsiders, Tarron was living the perfect life. He was known to be very successful at work. He appeared to have a wonderful relationship with his kids, and he had a drop-dead gorgeous wife. Still he wanted more. Tarron knew that he was wrong for having such strong feelings for another woman. But he couldn't help himself. At times he'd write his wife's and mistress's names on paper, with a list of pros and cons for each, as if to convince himself that their qualities would change. Secret: beautiful, sexy, great mother, sweet, predictable, boring at times, worrisome. Victoria: beautiful, sexy, spontaneous, wild, demanding, crazy, unpredictable, youthful.

Tarron had enough for the night. Constant bickering, a losing football team, and two masturbation sessions later, his mind was already on overload. He decided that a hot shower to relax his mind would do him some good. He grabbed another piece of cake before heading upstairs.

As the water dripped below his navel, Tarron noticed another swelling. He quickly lathered his hands with Lever 2000 and began his regular nightly massage. *I gotta see Victoria soon,* he thought as he released more cream.

When Tarron finally made it to bed, Secret was in her closet, changing into something sexy. The two-piece black lingerie set exposing the crotch was perfect. Secret had decided to forgo a bath just to ensure that her husband didn't fall asleep on her again. Since it was a holiday, she figured they'd have plenty of time for foreplay. That way she could put her new crotchless outfit to good use.

Tarron was on his back with his eyes closed when he felt Secret crawl into bed. A few minutes later he felt her hand massaging his penis. Suddenly Tarron thought, *Oh, this must be one of those frisky nights*. Tarron just gave a sigh, rolled over, and inched his body toward the edge of the bed. Secret snatched the covers, rolled over onto her back, and stared into the darkness. She waited, hoping that he would eventually participate in the scheduled lovemaking session.

Chapter 3

Tarron had a major burst of energy when he awoke the next morning. Every step he took had a purpose. First, there was singing in the shower. Then Tarron did an erotic dance with the towel as he dried off. Secret, on the other hand, woke upset, giving him the evil eye. She stood in the bathroom doorway, watching his every move. Not a word was spoken. She watched as he dried off his six-pack, pissed that he wasn't paying her any attention. Tarron began to rub his brown skin with baby oil as he sat on the edge of the tub. Even though Secret was as mad as hell at Tarron for leaving her hanging last night, she was getting aroused as his hands slid all around his naked torso.

Tarron was getting up to leave the bathroom

when he noticed Secret biting her upper lip in the doorway. He danced past her and around the bedroom as he threw on his tan business suit and alligator shoes. He tapped his feet to an imaginary beat while he stood in front of the full-length mirror, brushing his wavy black hair.

"So what's your plan for today?" he asked.

"Why?" she quickly barked at him and sat on the bed.

"I was just wondering."

"If you must know, I'll be right here after I drop off the children. Someone has to clean this house and make dinner."

"That's good," he replied as he left the bedroom and headed downstairs to have breakfast with the children. He played a go-go melody on the top of Terrance's head after he grabbed two Nutri-Grain bars from the cabinet. Finally, an enormous grin covered his face, as wide as a three-lane highway. He kissed Secret and the kids good-bye. Secret slightly turned her cheek to show him that she was not in a loving kind of mood. On most occasions it was the other way around: she craved his attention, and he paid her no mind.

Exactly forty-six minutes later Tarron entered the doors of the Viax Investment Firm in downtown Washington, D.C. He bought a coffee from the newsstand in the lobby and shared an elevator ride to the tenth floor with several of his coworkers. He said a quick hello to his secretary and closed the door to his office. With the slight touch of his computer mouse, his affair was in motion.

YOU'VE GOT MAIL.

His heart began to get excited as he hurried to click on the box labeled GUESS WHO? When it opened, he read:

Tarron,

Not that much time has gone by since the last time that I was in your arms. I can't imagine a life for myself if you are not in it. I listen to my girlfriends talk badly about the men in their lives and all of the silly things they must do in order to be acknowledged or included in simple things. These conversations help fuel my desire to appreciate all the wonderful things that you do for me. I know you belong to another, but you make me feel as if I am the only woman on earth. You make it seem like your only goal in life is to please me, mentally, spiritually, and especially emotionally . . . smile.

When those times in our relationship roll around and I know that you must spend more time with the other woman in your life, I'm not devastated, because I know you are planning some exotic adventure to make up for the lost time. When I brag about the great things you make possible for me, my girlfriends sit with their mouths wide open in awe. So, my Tarron, I will wait an eternity for your love because I know you will love me until the end.

Oh yeah, and you did please me last night, more than you know. My fingers felt just like the real thing.

Peekaboo

After reading Victoria's e-mail, Tarron wondered how he had ever lived without her. He paused to get the right words in his head. Immediately, his office phone rang.

"Mr. Chung Lee on the line," his secretary, Shanice, said.

Tarron huffed because of the interruption. "Send it through."

After he spent forty-five minutes ironing out the kinks with his new client, his secretary then barged in the door with a stack of folders needing his approval. By the time he finally got back to Victoria, it was her lunch hour. He decided to write, anyway.

Victoria,

Even though I'm married, you'll always have a place in my heart. Your soft lips make me feel so good. I wish I could have tasted those fingers last night as you removed them from your favorite spot. We must hook up soon. I'm feenin'. Please promise to do something crazy. How about never letting me go? Always wishing these moments could be frozen forever while we enjoy our lives without notice because it's wrong to do the things we do. Still, I hate to close my eyes at night, knowing that when I awake, you won't be there. So I promise, when she thinks it's her that I love, just know it'll be you in my mind and in my heart. Remember when we first met?

He hit the send button.

Tarron caught Victoria right before she left the office for lunch. She read Tarron's reply and smiled. She thought, *You know, my man is really sweet.* His response made her think back to their first meeting. Slowly, she drifted in her plush leather chair, thinking back to that crazy day.

Tarron was the youngest manager of operations for the up-and-coming Viax Investment Firm. He had just purchased a colonial single-family home on a two-and-a-half-acre lot in the upper-class suburbs of Bethesda, Maryland. A place where all the yards were manicured and the streets were free of potholes. It was a definite step up from his small town house in Suitland. The local school yards had swings in place and fully stringed basketball rims, clearly something he was not used to before.

It was a nice day, and he was out getting familiar with his new area when he stumbled upon a fancy little brick-front antique store not too far from his house on Wisconsin Avenue. He heard the soothing sounds of bells chiming when he entered the store, hoping to find something nice for the center table in the formal living room.

As Tarron admired a little cherry oak music box with gold hardware and deep markings on the cover and sides, he noticed a fair-skinned woman as she walked past the large stained-glass window. She was about five feet six inches in height. Tarron guessed her weight to be around 130 to 140 pounds. She appeared to be in amazing physical shape. She had long, firm legs that stretched up to a tiny waist. Even though her waist was thin, she had a butt that hypnotized him.

A tight stomach held up her voluptuous 36B cup breasts. Tarron lost himself as he watched her tongue glide across her full lips, covered in dark burgundy lip gloss. She had long, curly hair that swayed left to right with each smooth step she took. Tarron could not find a single flaw from what he could see. In one quick movement, Tarron was out the door and watching this angel of beauty walk into the bakery next door.

Focusing intently on her every step, he totally blocked out the sounds of the alarm coming from the antique shop. Tarron had exited the shop while still holding on to the music box. The mystery woman came walking out of the bakery as he was trying to explain to the owner that he was not trying to steal the music box but had forgotten to put it down when he ran out of the shop.

"It's all your fault," he said jokingly to the passing woman.

"Excuse me?" she quickly responded.

"If you hadn't been so beautiful, I wouldn't have run outside with an unpaid item." He displayed a dumb smile.

"I'm obviously missing something," she said, somewhat agitated.

"I was looking at this lovely music box when I noticed you walk by. Something came over me to get a closer look, so I came outside to speak to you. Then the shop's owner came out and accused me of stealing this music box. So now I must buy it to avoid criminal charges."

He moved in closer. "See what you and all your beauty made me do? You made me commit a crime. It's all your fault. Now what if I didn't have enough money to buy this?"

Her frown turned into a smile. There was something intriguing about him. "Well, at least you will have something to remind you of me whenever it's opened and the music begins to play." She winked, and not another word was uttered as she sashayed down the street, disappearing into the gleaming sunlight.

Tarron sat patiently by his computer, wondering what was taking Victoria so long to reply. With mixed emotions, having a feeling of excitement for Victoria and guilt about Secret, he reflected back to the day he met his wife.

The music was loud. The Panorama Club was jam-packed, with wall-to-wall people. Tarron was hosting his annual floating cabaret at the local hot spot. It was 1995, but it seemed like yesterday. He was sure of the year but wasn't sure if Secret had been invited by one of his business associates, another guest, or if she had stumbled across the event by chance.

He remembered how sexy he thought she was. The way the black formfitting dress hugged her frame. Secret was a very attractive woman. Long, wavy black hair with a hint of auburn rested on the middle of her back. She wore a pair of colored contact lenses that made her eyes appear hazel from afar. Her outfit and contacts worked well together, giving her a sexy aura.

Secret was a light-skinned woman with a rich, glowing tan complexion. Her arched eyebrows and designer nails were evidence from the very start that she could be high maintenance. Secret had an hourglass body that all men would label phat. Tarron knew he had to make her acquaintance.

"Would you take a picture with me?" he asked her.

She looked up from her champagne glass, gave him a thorough perusal, and said, "Sure I will."

The camera line was long. "I don't want you to have to stand long. Can I get a rain check for when the line gets shorter?"

She agreed. After dancing with several of the ladies he had personally invited to the cabaret, he noticed that the camera line had only a few people waiting. He quickly scanned the room and found Secret at the bar, chatting with her friends.

"Hey, pretty, you ready for that picture now?" he asked.

"I've changed my mind," she replied.

"But why?" he quickly responded.

"I realized that I don't know you. You might know my boyfriend or someone who knows my boyfriend."

"What does that have to do with anything?" he asked.

"Now, how would I be able to explain why I took a picture with some guy I don't even know?" She eased from the bar stool, as if to dismiss him.

That answer seemed to fascinate him. He wanted to expand on the conversation, but she had disappeared into the crowd. He saw her walking up the stairs, leaving the cabaret. Tarron chased after her. He caught up with her at her car.

"Can I at least know your name?" he asked.

"It's Secret," she replied.

"Well, here's my card. If something happens to your boyfriend, then give me a call and you can be the *secret* I never tell." She took his card and slid it in her sun visor. Tarron's mind wandered.

YOU'VE GOT MAIL.

He was happy to know she was still there. He immediately began reading.

Of course I remember our first meeting. Just thinking about it made me nice and moist. I decided if I was going to be moist all day, what the heck, I might as well take it all the way.

This is what made him feel like a man. Just knowing that the sound of his name excited his woman was the greatest thing in the world to him. Little things like that were what he loved most about her. The way she could be sweet but nasty at the same time. He thought if she could take it all the way, why shouldn't he?

Tarron began to unbuckle his belt to his pants. His penis was almost exposed when the sounds of his secretary knocking on his large oak double doors quickly made his erection fade away. He quickly typed *company* and ended his e-mail conversation with Victoria. Tarron hit the send button and stuffed his privates back in his pants. His secretary knocked on his office door again.

"Come in," Tarron shouted.

She entered slowly. "I tried to buzz you, but your monitor didn't respond. Michelle from promotions is waiting to see you."

"Give me a minute," he replied. Tarron couldn't shake her hand, since he had been playing scrabble with his balls. He spun his chair and headed for the restroom. After a little soap and water, he returned to his office, hit the intercom, and told his secretary to send her in.

Shanice opened the door, with more confidence this time, and motioned with her hand for Michelle to enter. Michelle briskly strutted into his office with a stack of folders. The two went over a few small concerns that she had about some legal issues and ended the meeting. Just as she was leaving, Michelle looked back and gave Tarron a strange look.

"What's that look for?" he asked.

"Well, I don't know if it's my place to say, but something strange just happened concerning your wife."

"Oh?" Tarron browsed around his desk.

"I just got back from lunch down in Georgetown, and I saw Secret getting into a cab."

"Okay, what's so weird about that?" His palms got sweaty.

"I know that's not the part in question. I heard her tell the cabbie that she needed to go to the court building. Tarron, I'm not trying to get in your business, but are you getting a divorce?"

"Thanks, Michelle," he said as he watched

her leave the office with a funny look on her face.

I'll be right here. . . . Someone has to clean this house, he remembered her saying. He picked up the phone and dialed her cell phone number. Secret did not answer. Tarron walked over to the bar and fixed himself a Rémy and Hpnotiq straight. He gulped it down and was pouring another when his computer spoke: YOU'VE GOT MAIL.

He went to his computer. It was Victoria.

Baby,

  I know you said that you had to go, but I really wanted to tell you that I miss you and would like to see you real soon. Make a little time for me pleassse.

Love me now

Peekaboo,

  My body needs you just as bad. But I was just told that my precious wife was seen in the downtown area taking a cab to the courthouse. She told me that she was going to be in the house all day tending to house business as usual, but I guess she had other plans. Maybe she's divorcing me.

He hit the send button.

YOU'VE GOT MAIL

Sweetie,
   It seems that her lying to you really has you tense. What do you say to us taking a long lunch at the Red Roof Inn and I ease some of that madness out you? I'm sex slaved.

Horny

Peekaboo,
   You always say and do the right things, but I need a rain check. Besides, I have a meeting later today. I want you to know that the next time we are together, I'm gonna remember how you were ready to go out of your way to make me happy, and I'm gonna repay you by sexing you lovely. Anything goes. Whatever you say, I'll do. Starving for your love.

YOU'VE GOT MAIL.

Tarron,
   You better believe that I'm gonna print out your last e-mail and use it as evidence when you try to back out of your promise. Don't worry about your wife. I hope she went down there to file for di-

vorce so you can finally come home to Mamma. Here is where your heart belongs.

Love Only Me

After Tarron read the last e-mail, he decided to call it a day on the e-mails with Victoria. His late meeting went well. He rushed back to his office to get his briefcase and headed for the parking garage. On the ride home, he wondered if he should even question Michelle's freewill information. After all, Secret had a right to change her plans. *Maybe I'm trippin'.* Tarron drove a few more blocks, taking note of the passing couples who braced the streets of Washington, D.C. Tarron pulled in his driveway, turned off the engine, and sat for ten minutes in silence before exiting. He entered the house to find his good housewife cooking dinner and joking with the kids. Tarron said his hellos and went straight upstairs to bed. He had no intention of talking to Secret.

Chapter 4

The next day Tarron constantly wondered if he should question Secret's whereabouts. *I'll wait. There is nothing like being wrong after jumping to conclusions.* He didn't want to open himself up for any long heart-to-heart talks, because it just might lead to her wanting sex. And, besides, it was Tarron's day to get together with a few of his childhood buddies. Somehow his brother found his way to be a part of the crew. This was the boys' opportunity to not only play cards, but also debate each other's philosophies on women.

Tarron enjoyed being away from the family on those nights. It gave him some alone time. Playing cards with his homies allowed him to vent his problems and compare them with others. Most nights after the game was over, he usually felt better about how his life was going and the type of man he had become. He realized that sitting in a room full of knuckleheads did wonders for his self-esteem.

He sat studying every man in his poker night group. To Tarron's left sat Pretty Boy Ray, the womanizer. Ray was a slender, brown-tone fella with several handsome features. He wore his hair in the traditional Washington skin taper. He wasn't a workout buff, but his body was firm and muscular. It was probably because of all the hard labor jobs Ray couldn't seem to hold down. He changed jobs almost as fast as he did his women.

Next to him was Kurt, the happy newlywed. Kurt was the red bone of the bunch. The guys always teased him about being one of those half-black, half-white boys from the baby boom era. He was the owner of his own urban clothes store in Northeast D.C. Kurt was working on plans to open up a couple more around the city.

On his right was Tweet, a manager at one of those Bank of America branches. People always told Tweet that he resembled the actor Taye Diggs from *The Best Man*. He was a short, dark-skinned bald brother with a little frame and perfect white teeth.

Jay sat directly across from Tweet. Tarron considered his brother a member of the new breed. Mainly because he believed he was entitled to have things handed to him instead of working hard and earning them the old-fashioned way. Jay didn't seem to care about anyone or anything. All he ever did was complain and blame everybody else for all his problems instead of facing the truth. The truth being, he was a loser—in and out of trouble since he was in diapers.

They had switched the location of poker night. The social was being held at Ray's new apartment. His two-bedroom, one-and-a-half bath sat in the heart of downtown Chinatown. The glaring city lights from the nearby office buildings reflected brightly through his living-room window. Moving the furniture against the wall, the guys turned the cozy living room into a sports bar. Black & Mild, Hpnotiq, and Rémy competed for space.

In the middle of the room sat a hexagon card table and five folding chairs. His large flat-screen Japanese television was fixed on ESPN. The volume was so loud, the fellas yelled to hear each other. This was testosterone heaven—music, sports, and a fully stocked bar were all the ingredients they needed for a chillin' good time.

"Man, I got this new girl, Linda. She's phat. I'm talking phatter than any hooka in a Nelly video," Ray boasted.

Tweet took a pull on his Black & Mild. "I bet she's not even twenty." Laughter separated the fog of smoke.

Ray quickly chimed in. "Nigga, she's twenty-three."

"Shit!" said Jay. "It's harder than a muthafucka to tell a broad's age by looking at 'em nowadays. I mean, I was driving down the street when I saw this pretty muthafucka, phat to death. I went around the block and caught up with her. I asked her name, and she said some shit. Her voice sounded weak, so I asked her age. The baby said fifteen."

"Damnnnn," the group hollered.

"Man, I hit the gas and almost crashed my shit burning off," Jay said, shaking his head.

Tweet shared the first philosophy. "You see, that's where God messed up. He should have only made a mold of man. He then should have made a store where a man could go and mix and match the perfect woman for him. Can I get an amen?" he shouted as he held up his hand for Pretty Boy Ray to give him a high five.

Tweet began pounding his fist into his palm and continued. "See for me, I want a black woman's ass, lips, and breasts. And I'll take a Latino for the hair."

"Hell yeah!" Jay shouted.

"Hold up, hold up. She's gotta have the

stomach and legs resembling one of those Hollywood white hoes, and top her off with an Asian woman's personality. That's the kinda woman I could keep around. And if parts break down . . ."

"What?" Jay huffed.

"Back to the store for a new update," Ray shouted.

"I found that in my wife and I didn't need a store," Kurt bragged.

"You talking that shit now, nigga, but after three hundred sixty-five days, year after year, with her ass, you gonna be like that nigga there," responded Jay, pointing at Tarron. "What was it, a year and he was looking in his old black book, wondering what all that pussy was doing? Three years when he had that drunken night and fell in some new pussy?"

Tarron wanted to leap over the table and choke his brother.

"I remember that. The nigga missed poker night for three months, feeling guilty," Ray added.

"And now this nigga's living a double life. He's happy hubbie by day and Rick James super freak by night. Look up in the sky. It's a bird. It's a plane. Hell no, it's Hubbie Ho." Jay had gone too far.

Tweet spit out his Incredible Hulk when Jay hit the Hubbie Ho line.

Everyone else laughed. Everyone except Tarron. He searched hard for a comeback line but came up short. He cleared his throat and tried to change the subject. "Let me ask y'all a question." He stood. "One of my coworkers was at lunch, and she saw Secret downtown, getting into a cab."

"So," Kurt said.

"I ain't finished. Earlier that morning I specifically asked her what she had planned for the day, and she said that she would be in the house all day, just cooking and cleaning. Should I ask her about it?"

"Hell yeah!" they yelled simultaneously.

Jay was the exception. He blurted out a long "Nawwwwww!"

"Why not?" Tarron watched his brother closely. A hush fell over the room. All attention was on Jay's response.

"Because you gonna seem like a petty dude, that's why—one of those petty dudes that have people watchin' his woman because he don't trust her." Jay paused and took a drag on his cigarette. "Don't be one of them soft brothas. Pick one or the other. You old-school niggas don't know nothin' about the game for real. You can't ask a broad about her indiscretions when you out there creatin' a whole new family. Nigga, you got a second life with another woman that she knows nothing about."

Kurt's eyes grew the biggest. See, they all knew about the tension between Jay and Tarron, but everybody tried to keep it under the carpet.

"Oh, hell naw, we not gettin' ready to go there, dog." Ray stood up.

Tarron motioned him to sit down. "So what you trying to imply?" Tarron gritted on his brother.

"I'm not tryin' to imply shit. I'm just saying, how you know what she don't know? Maybe she knows and just don't care." Jay felt in charge. "I mean, all the women you've shared in your lifetime, why would you care if she was gettin' a little on the side? Don't you remember the old days?" Tarron didn't like the sound of sharing his wife with another man. It didn't matter if he slept with other women—someone going up in his wife was a no-no.

Growing up in a single-parent home with Motherdear, the boys had still spent a great deal of time with their father, Marquis. Marquis lived on the other side of town, and the boys had an open-door policy. The only catch was to never enter their father's room if a red scarf was hanging on the doorknob.

The red scarf was the sign that their father had female company and they had better not disturb him. The sad part was that the scarf seemed to always be draped across the knob.

55

When the boys were old enough to comprehend what was going on in the upstairs master bedroom, they began to watch through the keyhole in the door.

Tarron and Jay got a kick out of sneaking and watching their father, giggling and making sound effects outside the door. Then one day, when the boys had come over to stay one weekend, there was the red scarf on the doorknob once again. But this time, to their surprise, the hole was filled. Their father had caught on and stopped them from watching. It was much too late at that point. They had learned all the positions they needed to keep the young girls coming back for more.

From their viewing pleasures, the brothers developed their own signs for pulling girls as they got older. Since Motherdear worked an extra job, Tarron and Jay had full rein of the entire household. This allowed them to entertain women as creatively as they could, on a regular basis.

Tarron's bedroom was in the basement. He decorated it to look like a small efficiency. When you walked down the black painted stairs, you found yourself in his small living room. He had put two small light blue and tan striped love seats in the form of an L in the far left corner. The love seats created a sectional look because of the end table that he used as the centerpiece. In the middle of the room was his queen-size bed, with his grandmother's old headboard against the back wall.

His dresser was across from his bed and served as his television stand. Tarron had a dark brown carpet that covered the entire basement floor. He added an eight-by-ten Oriental area rug to create a two-room effect. There was a short hall past the bedroom that led to the laundry room and backyard entrance.

All the windows were spray painted black and covered with black curtains so that no outside light could enter the room. When you turned off the lights, you couldn't see your hands in front of your face. This played a major part in the group-sex episodes the boys engaged in.

The black hole, as they referred to Tarron's room, was the perfect host to several games and tricks. The brother who was doing the entertaining would notify the other brother as to the type of trick he had planned for that night. He informed him with the same colored-scarf system their father used.

A blue scarf meant tag team; the brother entertaining had a female that was open to two or more guys at the same time. It was fine for the other brother to enter the black hole and join the party.

Normally, this was rare at the beginning of the courting session. It usually was the payoff after months of begging and giving scenarios of how special it would be and how much they wanted to please the girl involved. During that time, no female was off-limits, unless it was their main girl, and even she was tested before obtaining that title.

"Man, that's different. Those were just hos that we dated, but Secret, she's my wife."

"That nigga ain't no Hubbie Ho. He's bitch boy with a big *B*," Tweet shouted from the kitchen.

Everyone laughed again.

It was getting late, and Tarron couldn't take the heat any longer. He was ready to jet. No one really won any major money, anyway. His head was so clouded, he didn't know who'd won. But what he did know was that the winner got just enough to have a good lunch for one workday. Tarron sat and played one more hand before calling it quits. The joning never stopped. After a while, the testosterone became too much and brothers started peeling off. The newlywed was the first to leave. After another drink, Tarron decided he had had enough.

The consumed alcohol caused him to think of what he could do to Secret when he reached home, although he was angry with her. There were small flashes of lustful positions dancing about in his mind. He envisioned himself in ejaculating bliss . . . long snapshots of intense climaxing. And that was what they remained—snapshot visions. He figured she probably wouldn't want to do it that night, since it wasn't Wednesday. Tarron needed his fix and Victoria was it.

Chapter 5

Terrance's eighth birthday party was that following Saturday. Secret had invited the entire football team, several of his classmates, and all the family over to celebrate.

Terrance wanted to have his party at Dave & Buster's play land, but Tarron thought it would be best to have a party at the house and an old-fashioned sleepover. Tarron had worked hard all morning cleaning up the house and decorating with streamers and balloons.

Tarron's mother always did the bulk of the cooking for large family events. Everyone thought Motherdear's cooking was worthy of being served at the finest restaurants in town. Her fried chicken was legendary and a special request by all the family members. It was always cooked to a golden brown. The skin was crisp but not too hard. The chicken just slid off the bone and melted in your mouth.

Chicken wasn't her only specialty. She was known to fix a variety of dishes. For this occasion Motherdear had two bowls of three-bean baked beans, two pans of potato salad, one pan of tuna fish and macaroni salad, three plates of deviled eggs, one bucket of barbecue chicken, and three buckets of her mouth-watering fried chicken. Her car was loaded by the time she pulled up to the house and called for Tarron to come out and help bring in the food.

He was organizing the dishes on the table when Motherdear instructed him to begin firing up the grill because people were due to arrive soon. He quickly ran to the kitchen to uncover the indoor grill he got from Secret for his birthday two years prior.

Terrance's birthday party wasn't any ordinary eight-year-old's birthday party. Tarron had ordered all the special football decorations fit for a little prince. He ordered a Ninja Turtle to do face painting, and of course, DJ Musiq was there to crank out the hot sounds of the latest hits. The blasting sounds from the speakers were so good that the party quickly changed from a gathering of friends and family to an all-out house party.

The boys played tag around the house, the girls pretended to be mothers, and Tweet gave some children rides on the go-karts he brought over, despite the cold weather. Older boys ran a full-court basketball game in the middle of the backyard as the older girls cheered them on. The girls shivered as they pointed their fingers and giggled. Most of them had crushes on a few of the players. The adults nestled in a dining room corner of their own, shot the breeze, and played Spades. They joked about the dysfunctional family members, not present.

As Terrance tried to get away from being tagged by one of his football teammates, he ran straight into a familiar woman. He fell to the ground as she stumbled back, trying to maintain a grasp on the birthday present she held in her hand.

"Baby, are you all right?" she asked.

Just as Terrance shook his head up and down, Devin ran up and smacked him on his shoulder and ran off screaming, "You're it!" He turned to give the woman a disappointing look. *I can't believe you got me caught,* he thought. Terrance jumped to his feet and began to dust off his birthday outfit. For some reason he couldn't keep his eyes off of her. Another look from top to bottom and finally Terrance realized where he'd seen her before. He wasn't happy.

"Wasn't you the lady that was coming out the woods with my dad at football practice?" His lip quivered from the cold as he spoke.

"I don't think so, baby," she replied. Victoria had no idea that he'd remember her face. That was why she'd kept walking that day.

"Are you sure?" he asked. "The lady coming out the bushes looked a lot like you."

"You must have me mixed up with someone else." Victoria turned to see if anyone was watching.

"Sure I do," Terrance said, as if not believing her. "Well, all of the other grown-ups are in the dining room." He pointed with his left hand, then gritted on Victoria. He saw the other kids waiting for him since he was it, and took off running.

The music got louder as Victoria walked inside of the house and stood looking out at the huge crowd that covered every inch of the floor. There she saw Tarron standing with his back to her, talking with a group of guys. Tarron didn't notice Victoria until he heard her warm, seductive voice slide across his neck to his unsuspecting ears.

"Am I late?"

His eyes closed as his body began to tingle. Both palms immediately started to sweat, causing him to spill his cup of Hennessy all over his pants. Slowly Tarron turned and stood face-to-face with Victoria. He made a quick glance around the living room, but not too fast that he raised suspicions. He scanned for Secret to make sure she was nowhere in sight.

"What in the hell are you doing here!" he asked.

"I was invited by a friend," she responded.

"But why are you here?"

"I just had to see you. It's been such a long time since my eyes have seen your handsome face. Besides, nobody has ever seen us together, and with all these people walking around, nobody will be able to tell that I'm here with you."

"You don't know that! All it takes is for one person to see us together and it clicks something that will allow them to put one and one together." Tarron appeared flustered. He loved Victoria's spontaneity, but this was too close for comfort.

"You might be right. Your son just asked me if I was the lady coming out the bushes with his daddy."

"He said what!"

Just then Secret walked up and caressed Tarron's hand. Victoria moved out of the way. He jumped and almost hit Secret with his elbow. His eyes became distant. When he refocused, he was looking at Secret, with Victoria standing behind him. The sweat fell profusely from his forehead.

"Baby, I think you've had enough to drink. It's not that hot in here. I opened the windows all over the house. Why are you sweating like a pig?" Secret whispered.

"Secret, I'm fine. I've only had two drinks, and neither one was strong." His voice became high pitched.

"You must be the better half of Mr. Jenkins," Victoria said as she stepped around from behind Tarron with her arm extended.

"Well, yes, thank you. I'm his wife, Secret." Secret drew her attention toward her husband for an official introduction.

Tarron's heart nearly stopped! He never caught on to his wife's plea to be introduced. He could hear only the booming flutters of his heart beating through his chest. It then intensified as he watched both of them shake hands. Their mouths seemed to move in slow motion.

"Nice meeting you, Victoria," Secret said.

"And you, mister, like I said, no more drinks." She chuckled and gave him the usual peck before walking away.

"Tarron, snap out of it. She's prettier in person. Your family picture does her no justice."

Tarron slowly came out of the twilight zone. "Huh, what did you say?"

"Oh, never mind. Just relax. I'll be good." Victoria looked away. "Where's Jay?"

Tarron pointed in Jay's direction. On one hand, he wanted her to leave because he was afraid of other people's suspicions. On the other hand, he despised allowing Victoria in Jay's presence. If he knew Jay, he would try to push up on her out of spite.

"Before I go, I want you to meet me in about an hour at the park around the corner."

"I can't leave my son's party," he said, frustrated.

"Run outta hot dogs. I got some buns waiting for you." Victoria winked.

Feeling pressured, he thought for a second how he could get away. Motherdear saved the day, just like always. This time she rescued him down to the second.

"Tarron, do you think we should sing 'Happy Birthday' and open the birthday presents before people start leaving?"

Tarron nodded his head up and down and darted off to the DJ booth to make the announcement over the microphone. It took only a few minutes to gather everyone and have Terrance take position in front of his cake.

On cue, the crowd began to sing Stevie Wonder's version of "Happy Birthday." The children were adamant about mixing in the traditional song as well, so they sneezed during the pause sections. Terrance performed his same little silly signature rendition of the Harlem Shake. He even did these moves on the field. This was how he became popular. Everyone fell back in laughter.

Tarron searched around for his brother and lover. He kept it cool. To the untrained eye, his tension could never be picked up. "Oh, there they are," he mumbled.

Back in the far corner of the family room were two pairs of eyes watching every one of Tarron's movements. Over the crowd they stared at him—each with different thoughts in mind. Jay sarcastically lifted his cup and nodded to Tarron, acknowledging he knew everything that was going on. Suddenly, Jay began to grab his throat, making a choking motion. He dropped his drink, laughing so hard. Victoria tapped Jay on the hand, encouraging him not to tease.

SECRETS OF A HOUSEWIFE

Secret broke up the eye connection between Tarron and Jay when she stood next to her husband. Tarron slowly slid his hand down Secret's arm and began to squeeze her left index finger. Holding on to Secret allowed him to get a handle on his uncontrolled emotions. Feeling his wife's grasp relaxed him some. The sweat beads began to dry up, and his pulse rate was returning to normal. He turned his attention back toward his son. A large smile took over his face as he watched Terrance open his presents.

Terrance was so excited, too. He tore off the pretty wrapping paper to find action figures, a new soccer ball, some in-line skates, and several outfits. When he opened up the envelopes, all he did was snatch the cash out of the cards and stuff it into his pocket without reading or acknowledging who the money was from.

"Boy, checks are money, too," Tarron said as he picked up the cards thrown on the table. Terrance ignored his father.

After all the presents and envelopes were opened, DJ Musiq threw on the black family party anthem. "The Booty Call" came blasting out of the speakers as partygoers of all ages hit center stage. The entire house took on the appearance of the city's hottest nightclub. *Maybe this is a good time for me to slip out,* Tarron thought. Secret grabbed her groom, and they got their dance on.

"Honey, who is that woman talking to Jay? The one you couldn't seem to introduce me to earlier. You know that's rude. She had to tell me her name herself," Secret said.

"Oh, baby, I'm sorry, I was trippin'. I think that's one of Jay's old flings. You know he's got so many. Who can remember them?" he replied.

"He's gotten better, though. You see he didn't bring anyone to Thanksgiving dinner. She is a very attractive woman."

"Yeah, he really knows how to get the Halle Berry types. Don't mean they're worth a whole lot, though."

"She seems a little too bourgeois for him. What do you think?"

Tarron turned his head to locate Jay and Victoria. "You think so?"

"Oh, maybe they do look good together," Secret said. "How well do you know her?"

"Why you keep asking me so many questions about her? And besides, who cares about how they look together? You know my brother can never keep a woman. Even if he did look good with her, it wouldn't last, because he's such a fuckup."

The song had changed, and they succumbed

to the two-step. "Your brother is not so bad," Secret said.

"How would you know? He's been in jail for the most of our marriage. I'm through talking about my brother. I'm going to make me a drink," Tarron said as he walked to the bar. Victoria watched as Tarron entered the bar area, and wondered how she could get near him.

Seconds later Secret approached the table. Jay and Victoria were in the middle of a good laugh. "So, what's so funny?" Secret asked.

"Nothing really." Jay rested his cup on the table.

"We were just laughing at how children's birthday parties have changed. I was telling Jay that on my eighth birthday we were so poor that all I got was a bag of meat because my father was a butcher," Victoria said.

Secret let out a small laugh, but it was interrupted by Terrance's tap on her hip.

"Mom, is it okay for some of us to go upstairs to play Xbox on the big screen in the guest room?"

"I guess it'll be all right, but wait about a half hour. I think some adults are watching a movie up there," she responded. "Terrance, did you say hello to your uncle and his date, Ms. Victoria?"

"Oh, she's not my date," Jay said.

"She's not?"

"No. I just met him today," Victoria agreed. "Excuse me, where's your bathroom?" Victoria tried to make a quick escape.

"Um, it's through that door and to the right. If someone's in there, we have another one down the basement steps."

As Victoria headed for the bathroom, Terrance spoke. "Yup, I spoke to Uncle Jay earlier, and this is my third time running into this lady," he said.

Secret looked strangely at her son and then at Victoria. She said, "Oh yeah, when was the other . . . ," but before she could finish, several children ran over and began giving Terrance birthday licks. Terrance broke away and ran toward the hallway. She sought out Jay for answers.

He offered an explanation. "Terrance is so excited, he probably just means running into her three times around here."

"Oh," she said.

Jay convinced Secret not to trip. He pulled her to the side to discuss their plans on talking to Tarron about their sticky situation. Although the conversation got heated, he reassured her that he had her back.

Meanwhile, Tarron was in the kitchen, staring through the curtains, when Victoria came through the door. He didn't know where she had disappeared to after doing his best to read her, Jay's, and Secret's lips. It was true that he was concerned about Secret and Victoria talking, but Victoria being with Jay seemed to concern him more.

"Hey, sexy," she mouthed. "Where's your bathroom?"

Tarron was too nervous to speak. He couldn't believe she was actually in his house. He pointed down the hall. She headed in that direction. All the adults were in the dining room, socializing. Terrance burst through the door, begging his dad to get his box of Xbox games from the basement closet. Tarron ignored him, almost pushing him out of the kitchen. Terrance didn't like it.

"I'ma tell." Terrance paused, staring over his shoulder.

"You know what, boy? Get your ass outta here. I'll go get yo damn games."

Tarron headed down the basement stairs. He noticed the bathroom light on and decided not to disturb its user.

He fumbled through the boxes until he came across the intended games. He grabbed the box labeled XBOX GAMES. Stopped in his tracks. Victoria, who was standing in the door frame of his bathroom, naked from the waist down, caused him to drop the box.

"Oh sh . . ." Tarron could not get the word out.

"How 'bout a quickie before someone comes?" Victoria straddled the doorway backward, bent facedown. She wore no panties. Tarron instantly became hard. He couldn't think straight. When Mr. Happy got hard, the brain got soft.

He kicked the toy box to the side and ran like Bruce Jenner. Tarron released his untamed muscle. Pulling the hand towel from the rack, he stuffed Victoria's mouth. As she bit down, he went in. She held her position like a criminal on an episode of *COPS.*

Tarron's thrusts knocked her head into the wall, causing a small dent to form. Victoria never had a second to think. She took every stroke like a stallion. Tarron forgot where he was. Victoria turned to give him the signal to cum. He shivered like a baby.

"I'm coming, baby," he whispered. "Damn, I love you so much." Tarron clenched his teeth against his bottom lip and whined softly. Sporadically, the juice began to release. His liquids slipped down her leg onto the toilet seat. She bent down and cleaned him longingly with her tongue.

"I gotta go," he moaned as he gently pushed her away. "This is too wild."

Victoria smiled and kissed his dry lips. "Until next time," she said as she dried herself with the same towel that had held in her screams. She lightly tapped his butt as he jetted out the door.

Damn, how will I ever explain that dent? Tarron thought, fixing his belt.

"Boy, get your butt out that window. I know I've raised you better than that," shouted Motherdear, who came inside the kitchen to get more fried chicken.

"You scared me," replied Tarron. He felt so much guilt for sexin' his mistress in his basement.

"Ain't nothing changed. You've been married all these years, but your ass is still up to no good. If you ain't your father's son," Motherdear said.

"What do you mean? What are you talking about?" Tarron said, already shaking in his boots. He wondered if his mom had seen him.

"That's why I hit your father with a hot cast-iron pan. His ass had a whole lot of game until I burned the shit out him. That's the consequences of layin' and playin'," Motherdear said with a chuckle.

"It ain't even like that. Once again, your

mind is playing tricks on you. I told you, you was gettin' old." Tarron squeezed his mother.

"Now, get off me, boy, and stop hiding in this kitchen and put some more of my fried chicken on the table."

Tarron took the pan of chicken out to the table. There stood several people waiting patiently for it. When he put the pan on the table, he looked up to see Victoria fixing her dress, standing next to Jay again. He looked around the living room and saw Secret talking with the neighbors from across the street.

Tarron kept his eyes on all three pawns. Victoria appeared even happier since Tarron broke her off a piece. Tarron didn't like the idea that the woman he had just sexed was being entertained by his no-good brother. He got more and more upset the longer he watched them laugh. It was unfair to him that he couldn't enjoy her company. Tarron truly did not trust his brother, especially since he was aware of everything that went on.

After too many minutes of seeing them, Tarron became engulfed with rage. Jealousy ate through the pit of his soul. *Why am I tripping? I know she's mine. For some reason I feel threatened. I don't know why, because this isn't the first time a sidepiece was shared between my brother and me.*

Tarron recalled one scarf event. He and Jay had pulled the old switcheroo on a girl named Jessica. A red scarf hanging on the door meant that the switch was on. The brother entertaining would get his date naked, have sex with her over and over again. He would excuse himself to use the bathroom on the upstairs floor.

As one brother went up the steps, the other brother delayed a minute or two, then entered the black hole. This brother would slide himself into the bed and begin to have sex with the girl. This would continue throughout the night or until the girl was exhausted.

Every now and then the female would bust them, but it was after the trick had been played. Some females knew their body, and they could tell that there was a different size penis banging in and out of them. The brothers decided to have sex only in different positions so that the different size would be associated with the different position.

Tarron decided he could no longer watch Jay entertain Victoria. He went upstairs and found Terrance and some of his friends playing *Madden NFL 06* on Xbox. He took the control from one of the boys who were playing against Terrance and began talking trash.

"You won't score again," he boasted.

"Dad, you can't stop me," Terrance replied.

Tarron began to hammer Terrance on the video game.

Terrance got really upset and threw down his remote. "If you know what's good for you, Dad, you better let me win."

"Boy, you gonna take this spankin' like a man," Tarron said, paying no attention to his son's threats.

"I wonder what Mom would say if she knew about that woman in the woods being in our house." All the kids' eyes grew bigger.

Tarron grabbed him by his arm and dragged him into the hallway. "Boy, I don't know what's on your mind, but that lady outside was not in the woods with me."

"Dad, you always tell me to tell the truth. Just stop lying. It's gonna come out one day."

"Just because you saw two people coming from the same direction doesn't mean that they were together. I don't know why you are tripping, but don't get mad because I beat you in a video game!"

"That's not it. Besides, if that wasn't the woman from football practice, then she must have a twin that's good for you and Uncle Jay. The one from the field for you and the one downstairs for Uncle Jay," he replied as he ran away. He stopped before reaching the end of the hall. "I betta get anything I ask for, if you don't want me to tell Mommy . . . starting off with a new bike."

Tarron was about to run after him, until he saw Motherdear standing at the top of the hallway stairs. She just shook her head and walked back to the bathroom. He strolled past Motherdear, only to find Secret down on one knee, consoling Terrance.

Chapter 6

"Good morning, Shanice." Tarron spoke to his secretary as he sauntered into his office.

"Good morning, Mr. Jenkins. Boy, do you look rough, sir. Wild night? Should I get you some coffee?"

"No, I'm okay. Hold all calls for now, and let me know what's on the agenda for today"

"Got it. You have a videoconference call with the partners in Japan at eleven o'clock. Your messages are on your desk, and the anniversary bracelet is ready at LeBlanc Gold and Diamond."

Tarron nodded his head and closed the door to his office. Seconds later his intercom buzzed. "Sir, I know you said to hold all calls, but it's Mr. Jordan on line two," Shanice said nervously.

Tarron sprinted to the phone. "Good morning, David," he said in an enthusiastic tone.

"Just checking on the Goldstein project," David said in his baritone voice.

Tarron shuffled papers around on his desk. He wanted every answer to be precise. After all, David was top dog and Tarron wanted to always make a good impression. "Everything is good," Tarron answered.

"Good. Is that it?"

"Yes, sir. Nothing to worry about. I'll be out of town for the next few days. You know, taking care of the wifey."

David cut the conversation short. He always strived to maintain a business relationship and was never personal. "Keep me aware of any updates."

Tarron hung up at the sound of the dial tone. Slowly, he walked to his bookcase and opened a secret compartment that housed his private stock. He poured himself a shot of Rémy straight.

It wasn't unusual for Tarron to have a drink so early in the morning. Most times he needed one to settle himself down after a wild night out with the fellas. Between the party's setup, cleanup after the party, screwing Victoria in his house, and David's phone call, he needed a straight taste.

Tarron's eyes were glued to his desk before he could head in its direction. He embraced the visions of the hard thrusts he gave Victoria in his small bathroom space. Taking ten steps, he plopped in his plush leather recliner, downing the liquid from his Cancún shot glass. His eyes closed and his face frowned as the warm liquor went down his throat. He put the glass on his desk and shook the mouse to activate his computer.

YOU'VE GOT MAIL.

He highlighted the first e-mail address on his list. Tarron tapped his fingers in anticipation. The e-mail opened with a click.

Tarron Jenkins,
    I was wondering how you can even look at yourself in the mirror. How can you bring that kind of trouble to your own house? You've got the world in your hands. God has blessed you with a great wife and kids, and this is the thanks He gets? You wipe mud and dog shit all over your blessing. Could it be that you think you are worthy of having your cake and eating it, too? Well, you're not.
    Think about what you will do when all your bones fall out of your closet. What will be the reaction of your dear, sweet Secret when there are no more secrets?

Can you see her? Can you hear what she is saying? Can you read what is going on in her mind? I can.

You know she's fragile. Secret will be sitting in a corner on the floor in complete darkness. The tears will flow down both cheeks, dripping down to her broken heart. Thinking she has no reason to go on. Each day with your ass, she'll regret, when looking back at her past. Calling it quits—believe me, she'll think about it. She may be thinking about it now. That divorce might make the newspapers! Or maybe she'll kill you, then herself, too!

Keep living foul! She'll take your tail to the cleaners and leave you high and dry. You'll be seeing the light very soon.

No longer sitting back in his chair, Tarron was frozen like a statue. He hesitated for a minute before he opened the next e-mail on his list. It was entitled "Guess who?"

Tarron's head began to race. *Who in the hell is this? Did someone see me and Victoria coming from the basement? Damn, I'm fucked!* Nervous, he clicked the message.

My Dearest Tarron,

I hope it wasn't too startling for you to see me show up at your son's birthday party. We had a lot of close calls. If I could rewind the tapes, I would not have come to your home. You know I would never let our indiscretions come to light. The only reason that I even showed up was to witness you in a different setting. Oh, and to get some. My walls held way too much fluid. I needed a release.

I often find myself dreaming of what kind of father you are to your children. And just like pushing REWIND and PLAY on one of my dreams, you were in living color. It warmed my heart to watch you in the father-husband role. I never took my eyes off of you.

I wondered if this is how it would be when we are finally a family with kids of our own. Don't let my wants and desires frighten you any. I understand that we are not at that point in our relationship. This e-mail is only to let you know that in retrospect, me showing up was inappropriate and could have cost you your life. It will never happen again. I promise.

Thinking of you and only you, Victoria

Tarron sat in front of his computer, brushing his finger against Victoria's closing remark. The more his finger slid across the screen, the more excited he got. He paused several times at the words *only you,* and all he could see was Victoria's legs spread open.

Tarron's fingers found their way to his keyboard. They immediately began to type a reply to Victoria.

Peekaboo,

I wasn't upset to see you there. Maybe just a little surprised because I had no knowledge that you even knew I was having something. What seemed to bother me more than you being at the party, shaking hands with my wife, was seeing you talking and laughing with my brother, Jay.

I became a little jealous of the fact that my brother could make you smile and laugh right after I made you pant and scream. The minutes you spent talking to him had my blood boiling.

Tarron's cell phone began to vibrate. When he looked at the number on the face of the phone, he knew it was Ray.

"What up, fool?" Tarron shouted through his earpiece.

"We need to talk, now. I came up with a good business idea!"

"Business idea? Here we go again."

"I know, but it's definitely serious this time."

Tarron laughed. "Can't it wait until I get back from Aruba?"

"We 'bout to blow up. I'm about to make you a millionaire. Stop by real quick. I promise to make it short."

"All right, I'm on my way!"

He forgot all about the little note to Victoria. He told Shanice to forward all of his calls to his cell phone, and that he would be leaving for the rest of the day. He then spent a few minutes discussing the details of his trip, and what he expected of her while he was in Aruba. Before long, he'd packed and left the office.

Tarron was speeding toward Ray's apartment when his cell phone chimed. It was the jeweler's phone number flashing on the screen. He had totally forgotten that he had to pick up his wife's anniversary gift. Tarron quickly called Ray and told him that he wasn't going to be able to get to his house until later.

"Ray, I have an emergency of my own. I gotta bounce. I need to run and hit this spot before the store closes. I don't have Secret's anniversary present."

Ray instructed him to get there as fast as he could. His need was urgent.

Tarron quickly made a U-turn and sped down Georgia Avenue. The good thing was that the jewelry store was only a couple of minutes away in Georgetown. He was truly impressed with the custom-made bracelet. There were four one-carat diamonds mounted throughout the platinum triangular-design bracelet.

Tarron slid his platinum American Express card to the saleswoman. She placed the bracelet back into the gold box. "Will this be all for you today, Mr. Jenkins?"

"Actually not. Don't swipe just yet. Let me get that princess-cut diamond ring right there." It was showcased beneath the glass, underneath the box that cradled Secret's diamond bracelet. *Eight thousand dollars is a big price tag, but with all her tricks, she's definitely worth every dime and more.*

"This is a real winner here—one point two carats, F color." The saleswoman became excited about her commission.

"What's its clarity?" Tarron asked as he studied the ring.

"VS2."

"I'll take it."

Two charges later, Tarron was off to his next stop, the flower shop. Shanice had already reserved three dozen white carnations and a dozen yellow roses, to be arranged in a clear vase. Another swipe of his card and he was off again.

He had to make one final stop at his personal barber's shop to get a fresh cut, and then he had to make one call to his boy Ray, letting him know they'd talk business once he returned. Tarron was now ready to pick up Secret from her godmother's house, where she had taken the children.

Tarron walked up the long walkway, holding the large arrangement of flowers, and rang the doorbell. When Secret looked through the peephole, she saw no one standing at the front door. As she turned to walk away, the doorbell rang again.

She quickly turned and looked through the peephole to find no one standing there again. The doorbell rang for the third time. Secret was becoming upset. She yanked the door open, turned to her left, and saw the enormous flower arrangement rising up toward her from her silly husband, who was down on one knee, resting against the west side of the house.

The anger she displayed quickly turned to

surprise. As her hands went up to cover her mouth, Secret's godmother, Momma Mink, came out from behind Secret, cursing and yelling at the fool who was playing at her door.

Tarron stretched out his arm holding the flowers. Secret took the flowers and then smooched him on his forehead as she turned to go back into the house. Tarron lost his balance and fell into the flower bed.

Momma Mink just shook her head. "You betta not ever play with my doorbell again," she said.

When Momma Mink walked in, Tarron could see Terrance standing there, laughing.

"Boy, you see what you get for being a romantic?"

Terrance turned and ran inside, yelling for his sister. "Tika, Tika, Mommy beat up Daddy and dropped him in the flowers out front."

Tarron brushed himself off and walked into the house to find everyone laughing at Terrance's acting out of what had just happened.

"Oh, so now you're mister funny man. You think me falling into the flowers was funny. I'll show you funny."

At first, Terrance appeared somewhat standoffish.

But once the pursuit began, he loosened up. Tarron chased Terrance and Tika around the house until he caught both of them and gave them the tickle treatment. Secret loaded the car with their luggage as Tarron tortured the children. They hugged and kissed their children and bid their good-byes.

On the ride to the airport, Tarron and Secret talked about stories they saw on the news or read in the paper. They parked in the long-term Lot B of Reagan National and boarded the shuttle bus that had soon approached.

Minutes later they were pulling up at the US Airways terminal. Tarron called for a bag handler. The guy took their luggage to the first-class line inside of the airport.

"You two island bound, I see," cheered on the old black bag handler. They both knew his words were merely small talk.

"It's our wedding anniversary this coming Saturday, and my husband is taking me to Aruba," Secret responded. Tarron was not impressed.

"Oh, congratulations. How many years has it been?"

"It's our fifth year," she replied.

Tarron slid the bag handler a twenty. *Here. This is so you can shut up,* he thought. "Have a good day," he said.

The bag handler took the money. "I want you two to have a safe and happy trip."

Tarron looked back because he thought he heard a voice that sounded like Victoria's.

It was only 6:18 p.m. and their plane wasn't scheduled to depart until 8:05 p.m. Secret knew the lines would be long at the airport due to the new security guidelines, so she insisted that they leave extra early. Besides, she knew Tarron enjoyed having a few drinks before he flew to help calm his nerves. He never did like flying.

They watched *Kangaroo Jack* on the flight over. Tarron was bored out of his mind. The pilot kept interrupting the movie to inform them about the continuous turbulence they were experiencing. The two-dollar headsets were already killing Tarron's ears and now turbulence. He regretted even taking this trip at that point.

They finally landed in the capital city of Oranjestad. As he stepped off the plane, he needed another drink. Tarron was all shook up. The bumpy cab ride from the airport to the resort only added to his dismay. But when he saw the amazing white sandy beaches, he forgot all about his troubles. The warm, dry climate was just a bonus. Arriving at the hotel entrance changed everything. The lobby of the resort was lined with small rectangular tables, and casually dressed men motioned for them to come over and have a seat. Secret

SECRETS OF A HOUSEWIFE

headed in the greeters' direction while Tarron went straight for the check-in counter. He glanced over, only to see Secret stop at every table, gathering up pamphlets and brochures.

"Welcome to the Tierra del Sol Villa Resort in beautiful Oranjestad, Aruba," said the man in the homemade navy blue suit.

"I believe you have a reservation for me. It should be under the name Mr. Jenkins."

"Oh yes, sir, I have you and your wife in Presidential Suite one hundred."

The guy gave Tarron a cream-colored envelope and struck the bell on the counter for a bellhop. The bellhop retrieved the key from the man and loaded the luggage on his cart.

"My name is Betico, and I am the hotel manager. If you have any problems or need anything while you are here, just call me." He reached in his pocket and gave Tarron his card. Tarron could not help but notice his extremely dark complexion. Tarron was dark, but he hadn't seen a man that dark in his life. Tarron was taken aback by how white his teeth were.

Tarron called for Secret as he followed the bellhop to the elevators. Secret's hands were filled with everything from maps to brochures about Aruba's different beaches, points of interest, and dozens of tours and restaurants. As Secret came toward him, she glowed so beautifully. For that moment, Tarron wanted to fall in love with his wife all over again. The elevator doors parted and they eased in.

Tarron just wanted to get to his room so he could take a long dump to get the nasty airline food he had scoffed down on the plane out of his system. The bellhop escorted them both down a long hallway where only five doors stood. Four on each side and one straight ahead, which led to the Presidential Suite.

He opened the door for Tarron and Secret, and they were immediately impressed. Large Egyptian columns welcomed them as they moseyed through the foyer. Six feet away was the living room. Beyond the plush leather mahogany sofa stood four large bay windows that served as the portals to an immaculate view of Aruba.

Glass end tables rested atop dried coral reef stones. A hand-painted mural of the hilly, rocky island covered the ceilings. *What a paradise,* Secret thought.

Tarron paraded over toward the fireplace, flanked by two functioning waterfalls on the far wall. He turned to get Secret's approval. She winked in agreement. Tarron rushed to get rid of the bellhop. He felt revived. Tarron slid him a twenty and practically shoved him out the door.

Secret explored the remaining rooms, in the suite. She called out for Tarron. "Honey, you have to come see this master bedroom." Several candles were strategically positioned throughout the room. They were burning and giving off the aroma of wild island flowers.

"Okay, love, I'm on my way."

Tarron pushed open the white French doors with gold trim. The heart-shaped Jacuzzi was mounted in marble, and its crystal blue water was bubbling. When Tarron bent over to get a closer look, he noticed the blue lights set in the bottom of the Jacuzzi. The mood was definitely solid.

He was taken back by the bay window, extending from the adjacent wall of the Jacuzzi. The light pastel colors gave the room a soft feel. If the designers were going for the effect of having the outside world brought in, then they succeeded, he thought. It was a spectacular picture.

Tarron walked deeper into the room to find Secret lying atop the California-king-size bed. He tried to catch his breath. Tarron kept having radiant visions of his wife. She was stunning. While he desired to have that spark back, he never wanted to hurt Victoria, either. He was confused. It was as if he was seeing Secret for the very first time.

Tarron slowly walked to the side of the bed, allowing his index and middle fingers to glide across her exposed arm. Rolling over on her back, Secret adjusted her position on the bed. She lay gazing up at Tarron.

He opened the CD tray on the player that took up space on the nightstand, then ran to get his collection of old-school slow jams from his suitcase left in the living room. Barry White's "The Secret Garden" was the first selection to play. The sound filled the air of the luxury suite.

Tarron began to undress her, starting with her shoes. Although the complex formation of straps wrapped around her legs from her ankles to her calf muscles was no match, he slowly removed them. Tarron made it an erotic dance as he untangled the leather strings. This seductive episode lasted the entire song.

K-Ci's and JoJo's melodic voices assisted the mood as Tarron unfastened Secret's button on her jean shorts and pulled on the zipper until he could see the white lace of her panties. Using both hands, he wiggled her shorts off and threw them on a cream-colored recliner in the corner. "Forever My Lady" was still hitting the walls like a sledgehammer.

He lay down beside her and used his left hand to raise her white spaghetti-strap shirt so he could taste her navel with his tongue.

Rolling her over to unlock her matching lace bra, he paused to admire the garment that divided her butt cheeks. He thought of Victoria.

All it took was one swish of his thumb and off it came. He reached for the complimentary bottle of massage oil beside the bed as he kicked off his shoes. Tarron mounted Secret's butt and squeezed out a handful of oil onto her back.

Using a circular motion—the old wax on, wax off—he began to massage the oil into her back. The pitch and tone of her moans were changing as the songs kept switching in the little stereo. Tarron paid close attention to every part of her back. He trained his palms to stroke her back in a synchronized rhythm. The manipulation techniques caused Secret to feel warm and moist inside.

As Tarron focused his attention on the backs of her legs, he got lost in the lyrics to Keith Sweat's top hit "Make It Last Forever." He whispered the words to the song. Tarron loved the way Keith begged. It always helped him get Secret to give him some in their earlier years, especially if she was mad at him. She always gave in.

The stiffness from the airplane ride was gone. Secret was ready to have her man inside of her. She rolled over and sat up desperately. There was no connection between the slow song playing and the way Secret undressed Tarron. She tore his clothes off like a meat-eating lioness.

They both locked on to each other, standing beside the bed, slowly moving their bodies. The more Prince belted out the words to his song "International Lover," the more Tarron's erection grew. Secret's secret place juiced the string of her thong. She glistened from the strawberry-scented oil and the flickering flames from the burning candles.

Tarron lifted Secret into his arms and laid her gently on the bed. Kissing her inner thighs, he removed her last item of clothing with his teeth. Licking her ankle and all the way up her leg, he hesitated at Secret's garden. Inspecting her manicured vagina with his thumbs, he began to flick his tongue on her moist clitoris.

He expanded his tongue to lick up and down her entire vagina. Using his strong jaw muscles, he began to suck the lips of her vagina into his mouth as he massaged them with a humming vibration. Flashes of Victoria continued to take over his mind. Secret climaxed. Tarron sucked faster, licked deeper, until he felt her warm juices filling his mouth, overflowing his lips. He softly whispered Victoria's name.

Secret moaned with delight. Tarron frowned

in displeasure but was ready to insert himself into her waterfall of cum. Teasing her with the tip of his penis, he moved the head in and out, rubbing against her throbbing clitoris. Secret's nails dug into his back, causing him to thrust himself fully into her with great force.

Grabbing her ass and pulling upward on her thighs, Tarron began to press against her back walls. Legs were being raised, nipples were being nibbled, shoulders were licked, and screams were echoed. Secret's pussy began to grip his penis as her legs started shaking immensely. A second orgasm was a distant memory, as the third had come and gone, and the fourth was steadily approaching.

Tarron maneuvered her right leg across his chest, making Secret turn to her side as he sat upright between her legs, pounding her pussy to the bass of that song in the movie *School Daze*. Tarron was in perfect position to start smacking and caressing her ass. The stinging of the smacks was painful but in a good way. Her moans became louder and louder. Their bodies were dripping with sweat. Tarron wanted so desperately to enter her second hole, but he remembered that was Victoria's pleasure and Secret's nightmare.

Faster and faster he went in and out of her. The tingling sensation started in the tip of his penis. Quickly, it raced down his shaft as his hands clenched the pillow. Tarron's back arched as he pulled his penis out of her throbbing pussy and ejaculated with an abundance of navy seamen onto her torso.

He rolled over on his back, thinking he would have some time to recuperate, but Secret had other ideas. She rose to her knees and invited his still dripping but shrinking penis into her mouth. Her vacuum technique pulled more and more cum out of his shaft and into her mouth. His muscle began to stiffen again. Her tongue played magic tricks on his testicles, sucking hard on the left while massaging the right. Tarron was shocked.

The commander in chief gave his bulging soldier a new assignment; it was time to return to war. Secret wasn't going to waste another second with foreplay. She climbed on top of his fighting muscle and used her treasure box to grip his shaft to ease it back into battle. Without moving any part of her body except the inner muscles of her vagina, she squeezed his soldier at different levels.

This was the new trick she had learned and wanted to try after stumbling upon a *Real Sex* episode on HBO. Although Tarron's eyes were shut, Secret could see them rolling around beneath his eyelids. *Damn, my wife is turning into a wilder beast. Where in the world did she learn this trick? It makes me think she consulted Victoria.* Tarron smirked at his thoughts. Secret figured she was working him by his expression. Little did she know, Tarron smiled at the sound of his mistress's name.

"Hell yeah! That's my song," screamed Secret as "Forever My Lady" by Jodeci floated through the air.

She moved her body like a modern-day Jamaican dance hall girl.

"Whose dick is this?"

What? Whatever has gotten into my wife, I love it. Freak of the week . . . wow!

"You heard me. Whose dick is this?" she repeated.

Tarron was becoming even more aroused from her nasty question. It immediately reminded him of something Victoria would say.

"Baby, it's yours," he answered.

Secret put her mouth real close to Tarron's ear and whispered, "I'm gonna fuck the shit out of you." Then she began pounding her pussy up and down his dick—faster and harder, harder and faster, faster and harder—until they both passed out.

Tarron woke the next morning, sticky from the sweat the night before. Secret, nude, was straddled across him. Secret was awakened by the crawling feeling of what she thought was a bug, only to find the box holding her diamond bracelet was being dragged across her naked body.

"Happy anniversary, my love," he whispered.

"You never cease to amaze me." Though deep in her heart Secret knew things weren't the best between them, she applauded his effort.

They spent the remainder of the trip mostly touring. The first night there was their only real sexual escapade. They gained weight and bought a lot of souvenirs. They were forced to purchase an extra suitcase for all the gifts Secret brought back.

On checkout day, Secret realized that she hadn't seen her airline ticket. She searched everywhere but came up short. She thought to call the credit card company to get her travel details in order to reorder another ticket.

"Okay, Mrs. Jenkins, let me pull up your information on the screen and we'll get you straightened out. Oh, here we are. Well, I can say that as special as you are to your husband, I'm sure he wouldn't want to leave you there." The customer service rep seemed excited.

"Oh, he does love me. I'm blessed," Secret lied.

"Okay, well, I see here that you got two special gifts from LeBlanc Gold and Diamond jewelry store, flowers, and . . . Oh, here we are. Do you have a pen to take down the information?"

"Excuse me . . . Eric is it?" Secret stopped him.

"Yes, ma'am, Eric it is." He sounded a little sweet.

"What do you mean, two gifts?"

"Yes, two gifts, and going by the price tag, that must be an awesome bracelet and a huge diamond ring."

Her nostrils flared when she learned of the additional purchase from the jewelry store. Eric was not the one to take her frustrations out on. Secret collected herself. Playing it cool, she responded, "My husband surprises me all the time. He must be saving the other one for later."

"I hope so for his sake," Eric said before catching himself. "Okay, Mrs. Jenkins, you're all squared away. Thank you for calling American Express. Enjoy your flight home."

Secret gently closed her phone in a daze. *He said after the first time, he would never cheat on me ever again.*

When Tarron came back from the downstairs lobby, Secret looked through him with a glaring stare. *I'll give him a month, and if that diamond ring doesn't surface, it's gravy for him.* Secret pulled herself together and cuddled up close to Tarron on the taxi ride back to the airport. She held it together on the flight home. He glowed, and Secret didn't want to mess that up. *I hope I'm the reason he smiles.* She glared out the window into the clouds. *Please don't let him fuck up our marriage. I'm not taking him cheating on me again.* Secret turned to her husband and winked.

No matter how much she tried to block out her feelings, the mysterious *diamond ring* boggled her brain. It wasn't like Secret to challenge Tarron on the issue of how or on whom he spent his money. After all, Tarron made every dollar that came into the house. Every bill was paid on time, and anything extra was available to the entire family. Whatever Secret's heart desired was hers. All she had to do was ask for it and Tarron supplied it. The kids wanted for nothing. How could she question a diamond ring that he had bought when technically she shouldn't know about it? If she hadn't lost her airline ticket, the ring wouldn't have even been a thought.

What if she decided to ask him about it and it turned out it was a present meant for her at a later date? Motherdear was having a birthday soon, and the ring might be for her. She didn't want Tarron to feel like she didn't trust him. Secret had watched so many of her girlfriends' relationships crumble because they were out trying to find dirt on their men until they did.

Secret understood how relationships worked. If you looked hard enough, you would find a skeleton in everybody's closet. That was how she found out about his first affair. . . . She went on a fishing expedition. The fact of the matter was that things were going wonderfully after their anniversary trip, and she didn't want to destroy the mood, especially before getting all the facts. There was simply no politically correct way to ask him about the ring. So she decided to talk with Motherdear about it instead.

She called her mother-in-law the day after they returned home but was unable to reach her. Secret left a message on her answering machine, telling her that they were back in town and that they needed to talk.

She cleaned the house, although it didn't need it, to get her mind off of her dilemma. In the midst of her dusting, there was a sudden knock on the door. She opened it and felt her two angels' forces. Tika and Terrance attacked her like they hadn't seen her in years.

"Mommy, Mommy!" they both screamed.

J. Tremble

"My babies are home. Oh, how I missed you two. I couldn't stop thinking of either of you."

"Why? You knew they were in good hands with their Momma Mink."

"Of course I knew they were in good hands. That was just a metaphor."

"I done told you about trying to use fancy words with me. Just take your foot out yo mouth and apologize for being such a butt, girl," said Momma Mink.

The children laughed.

Secret patted the kids on their bottoms and gave a command. "Take your bags upstairs and play a little bit. You'll take your baths later."

The children ran off, tagging each other. Momma Mink hugged Secret and headed out the door. "You get some sleep, girl. You lookin' a hot mess," she said, grabbing the doorknob.

Momma Mink passed Motherdear on her way down the pathway. They exchanged hellos, and Motherdear walked straight into the house without knocking. As soon as she entered, she frowned at Secret, waiting for her to pour out her concerns. Secret shot her looks that pleaded for rescue. Instantly, she buried her head in Motherdear's chest.

Motherdear shook her head. "Come on, child, and tell me what that man of yours has

106

done now," she said, pulling Secret into the living room.

Secret sat down on the sofa across from her. "I found out that when Tarron bought my anniversary gift, he also purchased a very expensive diamond ring, but he hasn't given it to me yet," she said.

"What did he do with the ring?"

"That's just it. I don't know what happened to the ring. I was wondering, should I ask him about it?" Secret sat with a lack of confidence.

"If you want to start some shit, you should ask him. Why do you care? Is he cheating on you like his no-good father?"

"I really don't know. There have been several changes in the last few months. He has been working late a lot at the office. Whenever I call the office, the secretary is always saying that he can't be disturbed. Tarron and Terrance are having some issues that neither wants to talk about."

Motherdear scooted to the edge of the chair. "That don't sound like a man that's cheating, but the working of a man who just got a new promotion, tryin' to maintain his position."

"I know it does, but I just have this feeling to ask him."

"Where is Mr. Man, anyway?"

"Well, tonight is Thursday night, so I guess

he is out with the boys," Secret replied. "Come on, Motherdear, what do you think I should do?"

"I know my son. If it was me and his father, I would ask him in a heartbeat just because his ass was no good. I would just have to know. But Tarron is not his father, but he does provide for yaws family. Don't make waves with a boat that ain't rocking. Hell, I'm running late to play my numbers," Motherdear said as she stood and headed for the door.

"I guess you may be right. Maybe I'm just paranoid," said Secret as she walked behind her. As Secret closed the door, she thought, *Fuck that. I'm going do what's best for Secret, and if that means making some waves, so be it.*

Chapter 7

"Women ain't shit."

"Damn, Tweet, we only been here twenty minutes and you already complaining about women," Jay said.

"It's hot as hell in here. Can we at least open the damn window?" Ray shouted.

"I already did, nigga. Why?" Tweet said.

"Just asking, 'cause I was thinking that your breath smelt like pure ass when I walked in here."

Everybody burst out laughing except Tweet. He grabbed a handful of his jeans and told Ray to bite it.

"Can I please get on with my story?"

"Go ahead, little girl," Tarron said, studying his hand.

"Like I was saying, bitches ain't shit. Listen, you know that girl Jackie I'm seeing?"

"The tall, light-skin freak, with the phat ass?" Pretty Boy Ray asked.

"Yeah, that's her." Tweet took a sip from his cup. "Well, I was planning on making her my girl, but the bitch burnt me the last time we hooked up." Cards went flying everywhere. Jay choked from the beer that ran down his throat, and Tweet just sat there, shaking his head. "It ain't funny. I gotta sit and piss with one leg up," Tweet added.

Ray broke in. "That's why I wear two rubbers with these nasty-ass hos. A woman will have to have every checkup, exam, and test known to the medical field before I go bareback," he added as he gave Tarron a high five.

"Man, this shit was downright wrong. I was in a meeting at the bank when I had to piss real bad. I slid out my row, hurried to the bathroom, and whipped out old boy, and then I felt a pain like no other pain I ever imagined. I mean, I cried." The more Tweet told about his awful ordeal, the more the guys laughed.

"That nigga's dick is on fire," Kurt joked.

"Every time Tweet takes a leak, the fire alarm goes off," Ray shouted.

The guys spent most of the night joning on

Tweet until Tarron noticed Kurt flipping through his old black book.

"Hey, Kurt, trouble in paradise?" Tarron asked.

"Naw, I was just wondering what some of my old pieces might be up to now."

"That's how it starts. First, everything is wonderful, then the routine sets in, next you wonder about the past, and finally you question your future." Tarron shook his head.

"It's not like that. I mean, Cheryl is my life. She's the only woman that takes me to my chillum place."

"Chillum place . . . what the fu . . . ," Ray bawled.

"It's the rainbow of loveliness . . . where she takes me every time we make love."

"Hold up. Hold up. . . . Skittles, nigga. Taste the rainbow. That was gay," Jay interrupted. "You sound like a straight bitch. I don't even think a bitch would come up with some ol' bullshit like that." Everyone laughed.

Tweet was stumbling toward the bathroom when Ray shouted, "Take the fire extinguisher with you, you human blowtorch."

"Ha, ha, ha, Mr. Funnyman. You know you can suck my dick."

"I'll pass. Man, even if I went that way, it still wouldn't work, 'cause I can't stand extremely spicy Oscar Mayer weenies."

Jay's cell phone went off. After whispering, Jay told everyone that he had to bounce.

The guys began to roll out one by one just a little after Jay. Tarron decided to hang out with Ray once all the guys had left. Ray decided this was a good time to discuss his idea of starting his own business with Tarron.

"Hey, Tarron, what do you think about one of those Coyote Ugly spots with phat-ass bartenders that dance on the bar to the hottest tunes?"

"It sounds all right if you can find the right spot for parking and a system with stress-free zoning and liquor codes. And I mean some badass, phat-to-death bartenders to work the crowd."

"Come on, son, do you remember the crew of strippers that I had at Kurt's bachelor party? Those six strippers have at least two friends each that would be willing and able to set it off. All I have to do is pay for them to get their bartenders' license from one of those accelerated programs."

"How much are the classes?" Tarron asked.

"Hell, I can get them in for around a hundred seventy-five dollars each," Ray responded.

Tarron looked down at his watch and realized it was getting late. He quickly grabbed his coat and started for the door.

"Nigga, what you think about the bar?" Ray yelled as Tarron opened the door to leave.

"Sounds like a plan. Get some ideas on paper, and give me a call," he yelled back as he closed the door.

Ray's reputation for business was shaky. He was known for being very excited at the onset of a new project but then losing interest through its conception. There was the selling of lingerie and sex toys at house parties that he had arranged. That lasted only a month, and when every person didn't buy something and his profit wasn't that large, he stopped. Then there was stuffing envelopes—two weeks.

Next was the great portable car wash idea. He never even got that off the napkin, and now there were hundreds of portable car wash companies. Neither did the G-string home cleaners, the book about single black fathers, nor becoming an Amway salesman work. Tarron needed to know Ray was serious.

When it came to business and making money, Tarron was a wizard. He had no time for Ray's shenanigans. He refused to make a move until Ray did his part. To his surprise, weeks after his request, Ray presented him with the required paperwork. He examined the work closely and submitted Ray's proposal to his affiliates. Viax Shin Corp. saw the vision and immediately approved the business plan. They offered Tarron the funding for Ray's business.

The same day Tarron got the news from David Jordan, he contacted Ray. Viax Shin acquired an office building in the redeveloping area of downtown D.C., not too far from Ray's quaint apartment.

Tarron had worked out a deal to have a section of the first floor transformed into Ray's dream, The Lions' Den. Viax Shin fronted the start-up cost, and Ray was assigned to manage the bar with the option to buy. Tarron told Ray to meet him at Goins Restaurant on Georgia Avenue at 11:00 a.m. for lunch and a drink.

Ray was already on his third Incredible Hulk by the time Tarron entered the restaurant. Tarron was carrying a black bag in his right hand and his black leather briefcase in his left. Tarron walked up to Ray, who was sitting at the counter, and hit Ray's leg with his briefcase.

"So, what's up?" Ray reached out his hand. They gave each other a pound.

"Come on, son, we need privacy to conduct this business." Tarron smiled at the bartender as he headed to the VIP section.

Ray turned and slid off the stool and began to follow Tarron. He paused, then went back to the counter to retrieve his half-filled drink.

When Ray finally got to the VIP room, Tarron had the plans for the club spread out on a table in the middle of the room. Tarron walked Ray through the blueprints of the deal inch by inch.

The bar sat glued on 125,000 square feet of prime downtown real estate. The design included three unique sections. In section one was a large circular bar, extra wide, laced with marble and silver trim. It occupied the majority of the center floor. Exotic imported liquors were displayed on a box tower with lit rotation shelves by one push of a button from the bartenders. The club goers were sure to find comfort in the cherry oak, custom-made, plush leather-cushioned bar stools.

In section two, the Rack 'em Room, there were six professional-size pool tables, each surrounded by rich green carpet to match the pool tables' inlay. A large counter extended from the wall. It wrapped around the entire room for spectators to lean and rest their drinks.

Section three, the VIP lounge, was the virtual room. Each of the two sidewalls contained eighty-inch plasma televisions. The bar housed a projector TV that cast a large back-drop image, making the wall a large screen.

Ray's eyes protruded as the layout became a reality. He could see dancing bartenders, major fight night parties, and local radio stations broadcasting live from the Lions' Den. This was exactly what he'd imagined when he sketched his idea down on plain white paper at poker night.

As Ray began to read further down to the contract's fine print, he noticed his name on the twenty-first page, between two other names:

Tarron Jenkins: General Manager
Ray T. Monroe: General Manager
David Jordan: General Manager

"I see we have the same title. So what's up with that?"

"Look, you know your background. I went out on a limb for this idea of yours. I got my boss to put up hundreds of thousands of dollars to make this idea become a reality." Tarron shook the ice in his glass. He went on to say, "My name, my reputation, and maybe even my job are on the line. I can't give you full rein over this and have you not be truly committed. So, I'm gonna run the financial aspects of the club, legal and insurance issues, and you will handle the day-to-day operations. Is that cool with you, nigga?"

Ray knew that Tarron was no fool. The deal he offered him was sweet. He was getting his own bar with no money down and would be responsible for only one-third of the headache. Plus, it was true that so many times before he had given up or quit on businesses, but this time there was no stopping him. It would benefit everyone involved. Ray cleared his throat and was preparing to show his support when Tarron's cell phone began to vibrate.

"Hold up, Ray. Hello. You know, baby, you're right. I almost forgot. I'm on my way right now."

Ray shook his head. "Lady number one or *numero dos?*" Ray asked.

"Yo, man, that's wifey. Let's wrap this up. I forgot I had to run an errand for her." They shook hands and parted ways.

Chapter 8

Tarron arrived at his office the next morning with only work in mind. He rushed to open his computer files in order to send the updated changes to the Japanese overseas deal. Just as he began to open a file, he heard a loud noise outside his door. Tarron looked up to see his office door fly open. It was Jay. He slammed the door behind him as Shanice helplessly tried to get up from her desk to stop him from entering. He paced back and forth in front of Tarron's desk.

"I can't believe you," Jay screamed.

"What the hell are you talking about?" Tarron replied.

"You heard me. What's the deal? Why the fuck didn't you tell me about the bar deal you worked out for Ray?" Jay yelled angrily as he paced the floor, prepared to kill.

"Dog, I know this can wait until I get home from work."

"Man, fuck that."

"Slim, you are at my place of business. You cursing at me like I'm some cashier at McDonald's who forgot to supersize your damn fries. Have you lost your mind?"

The office door burst open again. This time it was two security guards. Shanice had called for them when Jay wouldn't stop, like she'd asked him to. All the loud cursing from inside had made her dial even faster.

"Is everything okay, Mr. Jenkins?" one of the burly guards asked.

"Doesn't he look okay, you rent-a-cop?" Jay stepped forward, as if to challenge the guard.

"Sir, I'm speaking to Mr. Jenkins."

"But, I'm talking to you." Jay increased his tone.

"Jay, calm down. Everything is just fine. Thank you for coming so fast, but I'm fine. I'm so sorry for my brother complicating your day with this nonsense." Tarron gave the guards a head nod.

The younger guard tipped his hat, while the other motioned with his hand for Tarron to call if he needed assistance. They shut the office door behind them.

Jay started up again. "Why didn't you tell me that you worked out a deal giving Ray his own club damn near free?"

"I'm your big brother, and I don't have to justify any of my business decisions or inform you of my every move."

"I came to you when I first got out of jail with a business idea for a teenage club. You told me it was a good idea with a good population, but you never got back with me. Then Ray comes along with an idea for a club with some dancing bitches on top of the bar, and you immediately find this nigga money and a spot."

"Hold up, slim." Tarron stood to set his brother straight.

Jay gave him no time to speak. "Ray, of all people? That nigga bolts on every good idea that requires a little work except when it deals with some nasty hos, and you back this nigga before me. Come on, brother."

"I've heard all you have had to say. Now can I get a word in?" Tarron asked.

"Go ahead."

"First, when you came home and you came to me with the teenage club idea, times were different. You had just finished serving five years for an assault with a deadly weapon in a drug case charge. You were on TV and in the newspaper. How could I get investors to invest

in an ex-con with a long list of drug charges?"
Tarron walked around his desk.

"Second, you were trying to hit a market
that is so unstable. Insurance alone for a club
with teenagers and young adults is enormous.
Summertime, Friday and Saturday nights would
be your only peak times, but would it make up
for the remaining months of the year?"

"But, Tarron." Jay tried to interrupt again.

"Third, the one sure fact about Ray is that
that nigga knows women. And when it comes
to clubs, making a lasting and profitable impression, you need a steady supply of women
frequenting the spot. You got to have women
and lots of them every night in order to keep
the guys coming in faithfully. I'm sure that
Ray will have the finest women in the city
packing the bar every night. He will have
women of all professions, backgrounds, and
economical status in there every night, spending that money." Tarron got even closer to Jay.

"Fourth, the way the young children are
today, security would be hell. If one bad fight
breaks out and a single child is hurt, the club
would have every child advocate group writing letters, screaming about closing the club,
and even picketing the front doors. Fifth . . ."
Tarron pounded his hands together.

"That's enough. I get your point," Jay interrupted. "The fact of the matter is that you

helped back that nigga Ray's shit and you didn't back me with my shit."

Tarron recognized he would be beating a dead horse if he tried to continue explaining himself to Jay.

"Besides, I know a rack of bitches, too," Jay mumbled. Jay was talking crazy at that point. He stormed toward the door when he realized Tarron was done with him. Just as he opened it, he looked back with a strange scowl. "You just remember that shit always comes back around, and, nigga, you're up to your elbows in a river of shit."

"Is that supposed to be a threat?" Tarron said as the door closed.

Chapter 9

Tarron entered the house, to his surprise finding Secret talking on the phone. She wasn't a telephone person. Even stranger, she didn't acknowledge his presence. He didn't need any more drama. His fight with Jay still had him heated. So when he got home, he was in no hurry to start up an argument with Secret. He went directly to his office in the basement to do some work. Tarron had settled in his chair and was sipping on a drink when his office door flew open. *What the hell is up with nobody wanting to knock today?* he thought.

"How could you treat your brother that way?" Secret said as she walked up to his glass desk.

"First, my brother, and now you! Is everybody going crazy? What makes everyone think they can just barge into my space and talk to me any kind of way?"

"That's just like you to try to flip the script. Why do you try to put the wrong you do on others?" she asked. Secret had not received the diamond ring and found every reason to snap at Tarron.

"I had a real trying day. I just want to get some more work done and relax. Instead of you being my brother's savior, how about you save me by giving me some alone time?"

"You need some alone time?" Secret turned, headed toward the bathroom to shut off the light. "We don't need to waste electricity around here," she yelled through the door.

What the hell? You don't pay no damn bills up in here, anyway, Tarron thought.

"And you need to make your kids clean up around here sometimes. I'm tired, just fed up with the way things go on around here. I'd rather get an outside job. You keep on taking me for granted." Secret picked up the towel hidden behind the toilet. The same towel Victoria used to wipe Tarron's cum from between her legs the night they got busy.

"And what the hell?" she continued. "Where'd this damn dent in the wall come from?"

Tarron swallowed hard. He tried to keep his composure. "Look, woman, I don't know.

Maybe one of the kids did it. You know how they like to throw balls down here."

Secret sucked her teeth. She straightened the floor mats and cut off the light. Staring furiously at Tarron, she spoke. "Say no more. I'm going out to meet with some of the women in our neighborhood mothers' group to organize our upcoming project. The kids are in their room. Listen out for them. Try getting off the damn computer," Secret said as she quickly turned and stormed out before Tarron could say anything.

Why is everybody trippin'? Is there something in the air?

Secret got into her car and jetted down the driveway. Tarron massaged his temple as he watched her speed around the corner through the basement window. *What's gotten into her?*

Secret didn't wait. She pulled over onto a side street about a mile from her house, cut off the car, and pressed star-five, then SEND on her cell phone keypad.

"Hello. Yeah, I'm out. Meet me at our spot in town," she said softly.

"Give me twenty minutes," a male voice echoed through the receiver.

Secret closed her phone shut. She checked her make-up. After touching up her lips, she turned on the ignition, made a sharp U-turn, headed back toward Wisconsin Avenue. It took her a little time to find a parking space in Georgetown. Finally, she lucked up and found a car pulling out, after going around the block several times. When she entered Marsala's Restaurant, she went straight to the bar. "I'll have a Sex on the Beach," she told the bartender.

A beautiful woman sitting alone at a bar might seem like easy prey for men. It had to be for men in the restaurant, because several tried dry lines, but she politely declined them one by one. She was getting tired of the schoolboy lines when the deep voice of a sexy man whispered into her ear. Secret knew right away that this man was different. This was the man who she'd been thinking of a lot lately. Tiny goose bumps rose on her arms as her heart slowed.

"Excuse me, are you waiting for anyone in particular?" said the man behind her.

"Yes, I am."

"I just wanted to tell you how impressed I was with your strength."

"My strength?" Secret asked.

"Yes, your strength. I watched the way you handled yourself as each man offered his best opening line. You never allowed any one of them to put you in a position where you lost your power."

"Boy, you are silly. I should be even stronger after listening to your tired lines of you 'being impressed by my strength,'" she said, turning around on the stool.

They went to the hostess and asked for a table for two. The hostess gave them a beeper and told them that there would be a twenty-minute wait. They took a seat by the fish tank. The two passionately kissed, pretending there was no one around. After thirty minutes of making out, they were seated.

They sat nestled in a cozy corner. Their waitress, Cyndi, was a young blond college student. "You look like a happy couple," she commented.

He played with Secret's hair. Secret blushed and asked Cyndi to give them a few minutes to order.

"Sure. I'll come back in a minute." She bounced away like a ditzy cheerleader.

Secret was having a hard time selecting her entrée. "Let's just get an appetizer and some wine until you decide," said her lover. Secret obliged and took a few more minutes to survey the menu.

When the waitress brought the first round of food, Secret decided on the chicken breast, corn, and wild rice. Her lover had the same. While they waited, they ate from the same platter of buffalo wings. Secret propped her leg comfortably atop her dinner partner's leg. He removed her shoe and began to caress her foot. Traveling up her leg, he fondled her special spot. Secret blushed. She always loved the way he massaged her.

"So tell me why you keep putting up with his mess if you know he's cheating on you? That nigga is foul. I can smell him all the way over here. You are way too sweet to be treated like you ain't wifey."

Secret looked away.

"What did he say about the charged ring that you or your mother-in-law never received?"

"I don't know. I . . . I didn't ask him." She felt stupid.

"Look." He raised her head with his finger. "I'm with you all the way, but you gotta start taking a stand." He shook his head. "What is wrong with you, beautiful women?"

"No one wants to be alone," Secret whined. Plus, she knew that she acquired her self-esteem, or the lack thereof, from her mother.

Secret's mother was very young when she got married. In fact, her mother's marriage was arranged by her grandfather. She was only sixteen when it happened. Secret's dad was about twenty. Ms. Shirley was a traditional housewife. She learned early to take care of the house and maintain the family. Challenging her husband on any level was not an option. Her father provided for the family, so he made all the rules, and that was that. Everyone had defined roles, very similar to Secret's household.

"I know, but you got me if you play your cards right," he said.

"Look, I know my husband ain't always been faithful, but I do love him and my kids. You don't understand that, because you don't have a family of your own." She carefully chose her words.

"You're right, but no one should be treated like trash, family or no family."

His words rang in her head. She had always promised not to be like her mother, and here she was, living the life she had fought so hard to avoid. Secret's mom had done everything, much more than her share. She'd cooked, cleaned, shopped, ironed everyone's clothes, helped with homework, and pleased her husband. The only difference between Secret's father and her husband was that Tarron seemed to appreciate her willing efforts to maintain a happy home. Her father, on the other hand, had taken her mother for granted. His expectations had been too high. Nothing had pleased him. Even when she'd been right, he had still been mean and cold toward her.

And to top it off, he always had another woman. Secret even heard that he had fathered another whole family when she was a teen. It amazed her that her mother never said anything, like she was afraid that she couldn't make it without him. Secret was glad when he died. But she knew that the way he had treated them affected her brother the worst. He was committed to a crazy home early in his adult life. She couldn't seem to visit him that way. Secret never talked about him. After she lost her mother, the only family she had was Tarron and the kids.

As Secret shared some of her past with her lover, he sat with his mouth wide open. "You're making all this up. She would have to be supermom to handle that caseload every day," he said as he drank from Secret's glass of wine.

"We all knew he was no good, and so did she, but she chose to stay with him. He never attended any of our school functions or extracurricular activities, because that would take time away from his other women."

Secret took a long sip of her drink and continued. "Still, when any one of us got in trouble, he would beat us with this thick black belt. His whipping was so severe that we would pray that he got hit by a bus on his way home or something. And don't tell me that prayers don't work, because that's just how he went. He got ran over by a city bus."

"That's a shame," he said as he began to laugh.

A few more hysterics and the couple were prepared to go. Secret's little *secret* gently secured her hand and guided her through the semi-crowded room. He made it clear that Secret was his by placing his hand slightly below the crease of her back. She giggled as she waved to the waitress. They strolled down Wisconsin Avenue hand in hand, thinking of their next wild hour together.

Chapter 10

A month had gone by, and even though Tarron knew that Jay was still upset about him backing the club for Pretty Boy Ray, Tarron knew he had made the right choice by observing Ray's behavior. Ray had made it to every meeting on time and had not missed one minor installation in the production process. While Tarron was busy with work and other big-money projects, Ray was interviewing girl after girl for the bartender and waitress positions. It was getting close to the grand opening, and the bar needed some last-minute touches.

Aside from the two overflowing toilets in the VIP section, and a minor technical difficulty at the DJ booth, the club was set for action. Ray was concerned about the girls' routine, because it still had some noticeable mistakes. Tarron and Stephon tried to reassure him and the dancers that everything would be just fine. They were only suffering from last-minute jitters.

Ray knew the grand opening of any nightclub could make or break anyone. And with all the work he had put into preparing for that night, everything had to be perfect. Not just perfect, but magical. Ray wanted everyone that left the Lions' Den to come back the following weekend.

All of the fellas, except for Jay, came early for the official lighting of the sign and the toasting. One flick of Ray's pointer finger and the bright bubble neon sign lit up the eight hundred block of G Street Northwest. Another flick and the water fountains flowed when the bar lights dimmed. The final touch and huge lights shined into the sky, forming the shape of a lion.

Just then, the girls came out from the back to take position at their stations. Ray called for them to come over so he could introduce them to the fellas. It seemed that each girl was prettier and thicker with each introduction. The girls seemed pleased to meet the guys, but were eager to get busy.

Ray called for Mr. Camera to come and

take a picture of the guys and girls to hang in the VIP section. DJ Splash was the first DJ to crank up his system. It gave Ray chills when the bass from the speakers electrified his body.

The room reeked with dancers. The girls warmed up to Ciara's "Goodies," twisting their bodies and bouncing their booties to the floor. The fact that their skin was painted with leopard designs surprised Ray. Impressed, he had even talked several of his dancers into performing inside of cages positioned on both sides of the DJ booth. But nothing compared to the elevated poles that rose from the floor.

"Ah . . . shit," Tweet shouted. He nudged Tarron to make sure he was looking.

As the thickest chick warmed up on the pole, the others were reminded to work the floor at all times. The guys headed toward the VIP lounge to toast once again and get ready for a night they would never forget. Just as they threw back the first shot, one of the workers paged the maintenance man to tend to a sink leak at the marble bar. Ray quickly excused himself to oversee the problem. The guys, on the other hand, kept drinking as the time was drawing near.

Tarron had paid for several commercials that were aired the weeks prior to the grand opening. They ran them during all the major prime-time slots. He had worked out a deal with the WPGC 95.5 radio station to broadcast live from inside the Main Event room because he made the Lions' Den the official after-party spot for the NBA All-Star Game. The game was hosted at the Verizon Center, only four blocks away.

Ray wanted his patrons to feel like real stars, so he'd ordered a long red plush carpet from a nearby Asian tapestry store. It ran from the curb to the large glass doors to give the real stars curbside appeal. Black poles with gold link chains added to the finishing touches. They were really for the *real* stars: when spectators and nosy reporters tried to get to the NBA players, they would be kept at bay.

The radio station advertisement promoted free admission to the first one hundred women and a half-price cover charge for every other woman entering up until eleven o'clock.

The line began forming at five o'clock. The doors weren't due to open until seven. The All-Star game was on all the big-screen televisions and most of the twenty-seven-inch televisions that surrounded the bars. Ray's dream was now a reality. Only 8:30 p.m. and all three sections of the bar were packed. The buzzer sounded on the All-Star game, and Tarron knew that it was about to get even better.

Tweet left the dance floor when he spotted Secret and her girlfriends entering through the VIP section. Quickly Tweet went running around the club, searching for Tarron. Secret was fiercely dressed. Her powder blue fitted spandex top left no question in any man's imagination. Men watched as her glued-on black jeans hugged her monster-sized booty. Even Tweet looked twice before jetting off to give the report.

He gave him warning that eyes were in the vicinity. Tweet kept to himself how seductive Secret was dressed. The lights flickered through-out the bar, which was the bartenders' cue to prepare their stations for bigger business.

The racks holding the fancy wineglasses were raised. Everyone in the club was in-structed to hold on to their drinks. Ashtrays and nut bowls were secured underneath the bars. A last wipe down and the DJ cranked up Usher's popular hit song "Yeah!"

All the ladies stepped on top of their bars and began to get the party started. The com-bination of the choreographed step routine mixed with freelance video dance moves was fierce. Some of the women in the club seemed offended, but the men were definitely thrilled. The lighting was on point. It hit every single sequence with perfection. The girls glittered with every twist.

Back-to-back, the limousines began to arrive. All the who's who list of the celebrity world stepped out, dripping in bling. Flashbulbs went off like fireworks as everyone tried to get the best money shot of one of the NBA superstars.

Ray was conducting one of his many inspection tours around the club when he noticed Victoria sitting in a booth with Jay. This night was going perfect until now, he thought.

"You are looking good tonight," Jay said, staring at Victoria's breasts.

"Well, thank you. I see you didn't go all out for this grand opening, like your brother and his boys, huh?"

Jay took a sip from his drink. "There was no need. I know the woman that I want. I'm just waiting for her to realize that I'm the man she needs."

"You sound like a man that's looking for love in all the wrong places," Victoria said, feeling uneasy. She had enjoyed dealing with his kind in the past. *I better get away from this brotha,* she thought.

"It's no worse than a beautiful woman like yourself willing to break up a happy home. You're seeing a fake-ass married man behind the back of his loving wife, who obviously cares a lot about her husband," he responded with a sinister grin.

140

Victoria's face turned red. head. "I have no idea what y about."

"No need to be young with me. We ar grown-ups and have no reason to be honest with each other. I know you screwing my big brother."

"Well, if you know all of that, then why mention it? Excuse me. I need to go before I say something I'll regret." Victoria backed two steps away from the table.

"You be careful walking around in here by yourself. I do believe that my sister-in-law is in here somewhere with her friends. I hear she's strapped," he joked. "I would hate for some-thing to get kicked off on grand opening night," Jay said.

"I was told that you were good with threats. . . ." She paused when she looked up and saw Ray studying their interaction. She locked eyes with Tarron, who stood stiff at the bar. He had also been checking out the entire scene.

"I hope you aren't using me as some twisted pawn in you and your brother's little sick, twisted game," she said to Jay before walking off.

Ray hurried over to Tarron. "Luscious, please give us the usual on the rocks," Ray said, reaching the bar.

The drink was intended for Tarron. He snatched his drink from the counter. "I just don't understand that boy. Why the hell can't he find his own women to play around with? Every time I turn around, I see him in my women's faces." Tarron was pissed.

"You wanna talk about it?" whispered a voice behind him.

Tarron turned around to find Victoria's breasts inches away from his face. He was tempted to bite. Tarron began to choke on his drink. He wondered how long she had been standing behind him and how much she had heard.

"Hey, baby. How's it going?"

Ray stood by as a decoy but purposely tried not to listen.

"I see my brother is up in your face again," Tarron said.

"Oh, he's a lightweight. I'm not threatened by him. Are you?"

Tarron loved her ability to remain cool in pressured situations. "I don't want to talk about him," he said. "Can I see you in Ray's office in about twenty?"

She winked, and Ray slyly handed Tarron the keys to his office.

As Victoria slid away, Tarron stared around the crowded bar. He took in the ambience.

142

On one side of the room, ⌐
brother. And on the other side sa⌐
harm's way. And even though he was a⌐
get laid, Tarron felt trapped and misun⌐
stood by his wife. The ticking of the second
hand on his watch sounded like military
drums above the music. Shortness of breath,
the sweating of his palms, and blurred vision
had overtaken him. If he could make love to
her in his house, surely the club wasn't a big
deal. At twenty after twelve, he headed in the
back to be loved.

While Tarron had fun in the back office,
Secret planned a little extracurricular activity
of her own. What Tarron didn't know was that
her hidden *secret* had sat four bar stools away
from him, taking in the entire scene. Secret
played it cool. She excused herself from her
girls and traveled toward the door labeled
EXIT. Once beyond the door, she made a mad
dash to the basement. Searching for her gift,
Secret could see his shadow and began to
smile.

"Damn, you sure do look good tonight,"
the light-skinned, tall, slender man said before sucking her bottom lip. Secret melted. As
she dropped her pants to her knees, she positioned her body for contact.

"Give it to me," she said as he pinned her in

the crease of the concrete wall. They could hear the people screaming to the beat of 50 Cent's "Candy Shop."

"Wait!" She stopped him to retrieve the condom from her Dooney & Bourke bag. "Put this on."

He huffed because he was ready to go all the way. "Please just let me touch it. I promise to pull out," he begged with his deep voice.

"Aren't they going to miss you upstairs?" Secret asked.

"This is more important," he grunted.

"Okay, I'll give you ten strokes and that's it." Secret rubbed his bald head.

Needless to say, ten strokes turned into twenty and so on. Secret lost herself in his eroticism. He handled her body so gently. Though he was smaller than Tarron, she felt fulfilled. He tended to every part of her body, and she loved it. She had never been licked beneath the crease of her ass. She could feel her voice rise above the bass of the speakers when he spread her cheeks like jam on a sandwich. He licked her middle until she sank into another world.

"What are you doing to me?" she screamed. Then the unthinkable happened. Secret tensed up as he inserted his manhood in her anus.

"Relax, baby. You're doing lovely." He couldn't hold on after three short strokes. Secret's tightness rocked him. "I'm cummin'," he shouted. His long legs buckled as he pulled out and dropped to his knees. Secret couldn't believe she had let another man do to her what she wouldn't allow her own husband to do.

He grabbed her, and they fell against the boxes labeled BEER. He licked Secret on her nose and squeezed her tightly. "I love you," he said. She lay silent.

Feeling a mixture of emotions, she raised her pants. "We better go now," she said shyly.

"Let me help you with that," he said as he put her hair in place and gave her another hug. "Don't be ashamed."

Secret stared into his eyes, somewhat embarrassed.

Her lover kissed her forehead. "Until next week?" he said.

Secret slung her purse over her shoulder and tiptoed up the steps. "Until next week," she said, smiling.

She eased back through the door to meet back up with her friends. "Where you been, girl?" Cassandra asked.

"Takin' care of a little business. That's all." Secret sipped her martini.

* * *

After Victoria worked his body like never before, Tarron knew he could no longer live without her. It was official. Ray's office had been consecrated and his salad had been tossed; that made both of them.

Tarron realized the feeling he felt once he and Victoria left the office. He had to do something drastic to get rid of it. He knew he could no longer live without Victoria in his life.

Amazingly, he hadn't even seen Secret all night. Coming from Ray's office, he spotted his wife on the dance floor with her girls. They laughed and had a good time. Staring into the eyes of his wife and the mother of his children, Tarron couldn't shake seeing Victoria. He had to make a choice.

In the midst of his daze, Jay approached the dance floor. It appeared that he made a planned attempt to get his wife's attention. Tarron watched as they left the dance floor together. *What the hell is that all about? Something ain't right with that,* he thought.

Tarron did not want to ruin Ray's big night, so he discreetly took notes. He threw another shot down his throat. His mind was made up. It was final. His decision was going to be the biggest one he would have to make yet. He knew that many people were going to be hurt. But Tarron knew it was time for him to truly be happy, even if it was at everyone else's expense. He was tired of living the façade.

Chapter 11

Tarron looked forward to going to work to get his mind off his personal life. It wasn't even hump day and already Dan from the marketing department burst into his office.

"Al is out sick, and we need someone to give a presentation on the new high-speed telecom virtual interactive disk. The Viax Shin Corporation board of directors will be here in thirty minutes!" Dan struggled to catch his breath.

There were several others in the building that Tarron could have gotten to do the presentation, but it was just the opportunity he needed to brush up on his own skills. He figured that he could practice for the more in-depth presentation he was scheduled to conduct at the seminar in New Orleans.

The presentation was short but powerful. He felt he needed to make only small changes to the parts that didn't flow so well. Tarron's staff demonstrated their approval with smiles and head nods as he headed to his office.

He settled in his comfortable office chair, basking in his successful presentation. Tarron swirled his chair until he faced the window. He stared at the clouds momentarily. *I think I'll take the rest of the day off. Perhaps I can finish up some of my work at home.* Tarron used to love to work from home. It allowed him to spend more time with the kids before he left to go out of town. The kids enjoyed having their daddy take them to school and pick them up, instead of waiting at the bus stop on cold early mornings. It had been a long time since he'd had one of those days.

Tarron swept his briefcase from the closet and hopped through the door.

"I'll see you in the morning, Shanice. Hold all my calls this afternoon."

She nodded and went back to her call.

On Friday morning the company limousine was running behind. Tarron spent the extra time chatting with Tika, because he knew that his time spent with her would soon come to an end. Terrance, on the other hand, spoke very little to his dad. He was still angry with him about the Victoria incident. Tarron knew the episode at the field was what started Terrance's change in attitude toward him, and rightfully so. After all, he had cheated on his mother.

It was a smooth ride to Reagan National Airport. Tarron enjoyed a glass of Hennessy and Coke from the minibar in the middle compartment. The driver called for a baggage handler to assist with the black leather garment bag and a container to store the equipment for the presentation.

Making it through security was the only lengthy delay in his morning schedule. He picked up two packs of gum from the newsstand, walked down the tunnel to the plane, and was escorted to window seat 3A. Tarron asked for a pillow and a cup of Coke with no ice—stirred, not shaken. The flight attendant seemed amused. *Nice legs,* he thought. His eyes trailed her hourglass shape toward the cockpit.

His ears were very sensitive to air pressure. Once the plane reached the appropriate altitude, he was fine. Taking on this new position caused him to fly more, so his fears of flying had subsided. Tarron made a practice of chewing four to five pieces of gum in his mouth at a time during takeoffs and landings.

With a slide of his company's platinum card, Tarron gave Victoria a call. No answer. He tried her job. No answer. Finally, he tried her cell phone. Three tries and three messages later, irritation set in. The fact that Victoria was seeing a married man made him wonder if she was capable of being with other men as well. A quick flash of Victoria bent over a love seat being sexed by Jay went through his mind. He made it a point to keep Victoria out of Jay's presence, because he did not want him to accidentally get his dick stuck in his girl. *I need a stiff drink,* he thought.

He quickly dismissed such notions. Instead of dwelling on where she was or whom she could be with, he decided to confirm his accommodations. Tarron spent the rest of the flight reading several newspapers on the Web.

It was a quick ride through the New Orleans suburbs and then a short stop at the front desk. A brisk elevator ride to the top floor and Tarron was able to switch to relaxation mode. He ran a bath in the Jacuzzi made for two and turned on the local smooth jazz station. His jet-lagged body needed soothing.

Tarron slept like a baby all alone in the king-size bed laced with satin red pillows. He hadn't felt that good since his last episode with Victoria.

The next day, before the meeting, Tarron checked the equipment and the wires. When everything checked out, he called down for a bellhop for assistance. By the time Tarron reached the lobby, the black Lincoln Town Car was packed and waiting for him. He whistled as he took steps through the lobby.

"Good morning," the chauffeur sang.

Tarron smiled at the aged white gentleman and slid in the car.

Tarron took in the New Orleans sites. The buildings and their unique architectural style engrossed him, unlike the style of homes and buildings he was used to seeing back in D.C. The ride to the New Orleans Convention Center was long. It gave Tarron time to mentally repeat his presentation. He stared through the jet-black tinted window in a vegetative state.

Everyone was impressed with Tarron's presentation. His impeccable style made him victorious over his competitors. Chest pumped out, he felt invincible on the ride back to the hotel. As he entered his suite, he noticed a small white envelope sitting in the middle of the floor. *I pray it's from my baby,* he thought. He ran over to it and ripped it open like it was a present on Christmas Day. The letter read:

Peekaboo,
    You are cordially invited to participate in a series of events. Carefully follow the directions, or it could cost you your life. Not literally. First, you must change into some comfortable clothes. Next, go downstairs to the front desk and ask for a letter under the name Scorpion.

Following the directions to a tee, Tarron asked the lady at the front desk for a letter for Scorpion. The next set of directions went . . .

You Know Who,
    Hail a cab and tell the driver to take you to the corner of Canal and Rampart Street. From there you will walk halfway down the block to the alley on your left side, near Blue Al's Restaurant. Turn down the alley, and find your next envelope taped to the back of a large black Dumpster.

Without hesitation, he was off. Arriving in the alley ten minutes later, he opened the next clue. Inside, the note read . . .

Knock, Knock,
    Bang four times only on the green metal door to your right. Ask the doorman for a brown bag. He will direct you to the service elevator. Take it to the eighth floor. While on the

elevator, open the bag and put on what's in-
side. Go to room 812. Knock four times.

Standing in front of room 812 in a crown
and a white robe with purple trim, Tarron
knocked four times. He felt stupid standing
there in the silly costume. He couldn't bring
himself to change in the elevator, so he had
used the stairwell for his superhero change.

The door opened, and to his delight, a vision of loveliness stood before him, dressed as
an Egyptian slave. The blouse and pants were
a sheer light purple, which exposed her lace
bra and panties. There was a white veil covering her face. . . . Through the veil, a pair of seductive eyes added a sense of mystery.

He could see himself in her glossy eyes.
Right away his heart raced. Only one woman
was able to affect him this way. The only word
he could muster up to say was, "Wow!

"How did you know I would be here? How
did you accomplish this maze? How did you
find this place?" These were just some of the
questions that came bursting out as she closed
the door behind him.

"Well, when I saw your name in the list of
presenters, I talked my boss into paying my
expenses and signed up for your presentation," she said. "And as for this place, it is
called the Pleasure Palace. I stumbled across

it on the Internet the first time I came to New Orleans for business. This is a place where your fantasies become reality." She smiled.

She continued. "Each floor has its own theme. The second floor is the movie floor. You can choose anything from *The Lion King* to *Star Wars*. The fifth floor is the wild floor. It's the one with animals. I mean a real zoo out back. This, naturally, is my favorite, a pharaoh from ancient Egypt."

I've made the right choice, he thought as he embraced her tightly. "Victoria, you are the true one for me. I'm leaving my wife for you."

She blushed. Victoria took Tarron over to the fountain in the far corner, the running Nile. She took his hand and pulled him down to the small rocks around the Nile. Slowly, she lifted his right foot and began washing it underneath the flowing water. Using a thick white towel, she softly began drying it off. Victoria repeated the process with his left foot.

After she finished drying off his feet, she escorted him to a pile of large pillows on the floor. Tarron sat down once again. This time she lowered his head onto her lap and began feeding him grapes, sliced oranges, and chunks of pineapple. Victoria was ready for Tarron to be inside her. She pulled his face toward her body and exposed her breast, and

Tarron quickly wrapped his mouth around her nipple.

He used his weight to push her on her back and crawled his way on top of her. Every part of her flesh that lay underneath the Egyptian slave garment boiled with passion. He tore away the thin robes and inserted his thick shaft inside her. Changing his mind, Tarron pulled out and headed down south for some much-needed dining. He moved his tongue up and down her outer walls. More rapidly, Tarron swirled his tongue in a twirling motion, massaging her excited clit.

Victoria lowered her eyes to see his face and smiled at his skills. She pressed his head deeper in her cave. Needing air, Tarron tried to pull back, but Victoria locked him tightly around the head with her legs. Since it felt good to her, she moved her pelvis up and down, taking his head for a ride.

After tasting her gooey fluids, Tarron yanked back his head to gasp for air. More cum squirted onto his face as he moved out. Pleased with his work, Tarron gripped Victoria by the ankles and flipped her onto her stomach. Victoria hurriedly assumed the doggystyle position. Tarron took a dive in her like a professional swimmer.

"Aah," she moaned. "Right there, baby."

Tarron lost his staff deep in her stomach. Massaging his balls was the ultimate.

"Damn, baby," he shouted, grabbing the back of her hair. The wetness and the force of his strokes caused Tarron to slip out of her.

"Hurry. Put it back in, shit," Victoria cried.

He rammed his penis in her again, prepared to get his nut off. They sexed until they both passed out. He almost overslept the next morning.

While Tarron was away, Secret had some of her own business to tend to. Secret sat staring into the oval-shaped eyes of the man sitting across the table from her. She didn't know how she should feel. She felt something strange brewing. Slowly, she took a large gulp of her red wine as she wondered why she was doing this to herself. This had become her usual meeting place—Houston's restaurant in Georgetown. Could this be why her husband was no longer interested in her the way she wished? Was it payback for her own secrets?

"You haven't touched your Hawaiian steak," said a passing waiter. "Is it to your taste?"

"Yeah, it's fine. I'm really not that hungry." She raked her fork against the thick ground beef.

"Secret, I just can't keep this bottled up inside me anymore," the man's voice whispered.

"You have to, or else it'll hurt too many people if you open this can of worms."

"If the shoe were on the other foot, I would want to know. It would kill me if I had to hear this through the grapevine." He lacked patience.

"Look, I already know I'm losing my husband to some home wrecker. I can't risk not being able to get him back at all. You cannot let this out in the open. There are too many lives at stake." Secret reached over and grabbed his right hand. "You gotta promise me that you won't say a word. We can keep what we have a *secret* as long as you don't tell about our big bundle."

He rubbed her gently on her cheek.

Passing by, Motherdear spotted Secret through the restaurant window. Her first reaction was to join her for lunch, but then she noticed that Secret was not alone. She positioned herself in front of the menu taped to the glass to get a closer view of the man with whom she dined. *That sure ain't my son Tarron,* she thought. The young man was too light. *Now, how am I going to handle this?*

Motherdear made a point to stay out of their business, but this had gone too far. First, Tarron, now Secret cheating. Their relationship was spinning out of control. She noticed Secret's hands trapped beneath the table and decided she had seen enough. Motherdear decided to confront her face-to-face. As Motherdear strolled past the greeter, she fixed her hand on her hip, ready for action. She wasn't prepared for what she was about to witness. With her back toward Motherdear, Secret had not a clue as to who was coming. The man watched as she headed their way.

"Oh, my word, haven't you two had enough?" Motherdear grabbed a chair from a nearby table and sat down.

The tears began to quickly flow down Secret's face. "Promise me that you won't say a thing, Motherdear."

"Boy, your brother gon' kill you." Motherdear stretched her finger close to his face.

"Look, Ma, we trying to work through how to tell Tarron. That's it. Nothing more," Jay replied.

Motherdear crossed her eyes. "I know both of yaw got a reason or two to get back at Tee. Please don't do nothin' dirty. Just promise me yaw gon' handle this, before things really get messy," Motherdear said as she pushed the chair back. "It'll hurt Terrance."

"We promise," he said, shaking his head up and down.

* * *

Tarron's night of enchantment affected his second-day presentation. Stumbling over simple words and phrases, and having to correct several errors he quoted when dealing with numerical facts, blew his high. It was truly not the award-winning presentation from the previous day, but he did a good enough job to win over the big money people in his audience.

When Tarron returned to his hotel, another message was waiting for him at the front desk. The overwhelming anticipation of what new adventure his lover would send him on made it hard for him to open the sealed letter. Physically tired, he took his time. He slipped the note in his suit jacket pocket and headed for the elevator.

Tarron rode the elevator up to his suite. He was in no rush. It was still early. To prolong his ride, he pushed every button; this was his way of killing time. The elevator bell dinged, and the doors opened on the second floor. Standing there was an older white man with a younger Hispanic woman. Inside his mind, the paintbrushes worked hard at creating a scene. *Tax lawyer, young secretary, remote hotel for some hot, butt-naked sex, or else threatening termination letter, dirty old man,* he thought. They waited for the next elevator. Tarron could imagine why.

No excitement on the next four floors. He simply enjoyed the scenery. Oddly, when the doors parted on the seventh floor, he noticed a little girl with her mother, who seemed to have been abused. Tarron's pleasant attitude turned to sorrow. The woman had made a bad attempt at hiding her bruised eye with extra coats of make-up. Inside he instantly thought about Secret. *As bad as I want to leave, I would never put my hands on my wife. If I can't love her, then I have to leave her. Ooh, and if any man ever put his hands on my baby girl, Tika . . .*

He had a heart for children. Tarron wanted to take both of them in his arms and let them know that they did the right thing by leaving. "Hold on to the good times," he wanted to say. Tarron smiled as the elevator moved. *Remember the first date, the wedding day, the birth of your daughter,* he thought.

The woman lowered her head in shame. It was as if she knew what he was thinking. "Take care of yourself," he said. " 'Cause being a punching bag is not what God made women for." Then he thought, *Is cheating on my wife and wanting to leave my family any better?*

His ride wasn't so fun anymore. The exciting journey became a stressful one. Tarron's depression came over him again. The lit numbers were fading off the elevator panel one at a time. When the last light clicked off and the final ding sounded, Tarron stumbled through the doors, trudged down the plush carpet, and inserted his card to his room. The light on the door's keypad turned green, and he used his right shoulder to ease the door open. Tarron collapsed onto his king-size sleigh bed.

Exhausted, but needing to be wooed, he ripped open the envelope.

Tarron,

It's been almost two days and we have not heard from you. What? They got you tied up in New Orleans? Come up for air so you can talk to your family. Sorry, baby, if it seems like I'm fussing. We miss you, and we love you. Call us.

Secret

He was able to kick off only the right shoe when the hotel phone blasted.

It was Secret. "Did you get my message?" she asked.

"I just read it. I was planning to call the children after I took a bath and relaxed," he mumbled.

"I'm sorry for tripping in the letter, but . . ."

"It's really not that serious, trust me." Tarron yawned into the phone.

"Would you like to call me back later?"

"No. It is good to hear your voice." Secret could hear the lack of enthusiasm in his voice. "I miss the kids and you, too," he said dryly. "After two exhausting days in these tiresome workshops, I'm beat," he added. Tarron felt sentimental after the elevator scene but didn't come off like he cared.

"You can always come home," Secret said, waiting for a response.

Tarron was silent. He didn't like the sounds of her words, since he truly wanted to be with Victoria.

"So how was your workshop?" She broke the stillness.

"Well, I think I did an outstanding job. I mean, I put everything I had into the delivery of my presentation. My back and legs are so sore."

"From what?"

"You know your husband is a perfectionist. I kept hammering out my work until it was faultless." He smirked.

"So you really gave it your all?"

"And then some. But what's going on at home?"

"I was able to get a lot done around the house because your mother took the kids out for some ice cream."

"Did you call her, or did she call you?"

"You know, I really don't remember who called who. We were on the phone and she heard them in the background, and out of the blue, she said she was on her way over to take them out for a treat."

Secret was about to ask another question when Tarron asked her what she was wearing. After fumbling ol' boy, he was getting hot.

"Huh, uh, a T-shirt and panties. Why?" Secret had turned into a freak. She wanted her husband, but not nearly as much as she did her mystery man.

"What color?" he prodded.

"Well, I have a white T-shirt with the number ninety-three written in yellow and purple bubble letters. My panties are the green thigh-high cut."

"One of the ones I told you to buy off the Internet?"

"Yeah, one of the ones you told me to buy. Undress and tell me what you're wearing for me."

"I'm taking off my gray suit with the dark pinstripes. I kicked off one of my black, white, gray snake-skinned shoes. I'm down to just my tie and underwear."

The last time they had phone sex was back when they were in their courting days. Tarron was feeling himself and wondering if Secret was doing the same.

Secret could hear the slight moans from Tarron as he made upward and downward movements on his shaft. There were frequent pauses in between his words. Secret figured this was another opportunity to maybe save their marriage.

Tarron's replies became delayed. Visions of Victoria were on a full screen beneath his eyelids. Secret's soft, seductive voice was fueling his home movie. Tarron's dry palm became maddening.

"Hold on, Secret." Tarron searched his carry-on bag and then his suitcase, but neither one had his bottle of lotion. He knew he needed something to assist him with releasing the demons from within. Tarron returned to the phone.

"It's about time," Secret said. "Did you find what you were looking for?"

Tarron used the complimentary sample of hair conditioner. His breathing began to slow down. It got heavier and came in short spurts. The most he could muster up was, "Uh, yeah."

"You started without me?" she asked.

"Please don't tell me you didn't know. Has it been that long? Baby, come on. I have to exercise the one-eyed snake." Tarron added a tension-easing joke. "Secret, if Jack was on the roof and needed help, would you *help jack off*?"

"If your one-eyed snake is Jack, of course, I will help you *jack off!*"

Tarron snuggled down more on the tan and white love seat in his room. He opened his pants to expose his entire manhood. Another squeeze to the sample bottle and Tarron was ready.

Lying on the love seat, with his right hand sliding up and down his shaft, Tarron asked if she was wet.

"I'm using my right two fingers on my spot in a slow, firm circular motion. My other hand is massaging my breast and nipple."

"Are your nipples hard?"

"Baby, they're hard as shit. Now I'm switching to my other breast, gently squeezing it with my palm and pinching my nipple between my fingers."

Tarron could feel his penis moving around and around on Secret's clit. He needed to be inside her. He longed to feel her walls embrace him as he moved in and out of her.

"Slide your finger inside you. Allow me to penetrate you," Tarron said. He could hear the slight moans of delight in his ear. "Now another one," he added.

Secret asked him if he felt how wet she was.

His only reply was, "I love you, I love you so much."

Only moments ago he'd had visions of

Victoria in his mind, but Secret was evidently in his heart. Phone sex for them had been a major part of the dating process. It had happened at least once or twice a week.

By the time Secret was getting ready for her orgasm, she was interrupted by the sounds of the children banging and screaming at the bedroom door. Tarron could hear the screams through the phone, but he didn't mind, because he was working on his second.

"Shit! All I needed was five more minutes with this bullet and—"

"Oh yeah!" broke in Tarron as he hit his second climax.

"You selfish-ass nigga," shouted Secret. *It's okay. I'll get mine tonight.*

"My bad," he said. Tarron then heard Secret yelling to the kids that she'd be right there. He softly mumbled, "Good night, love," and quickly ended the call. Secret had a large part of his heart, but Victoria took control of his body. He rolled over, falling fast asleep, and Secret rolled out for the night.

She convinced her next-door neighbor to baby-sit the children for a few hours. Seventeen-year-old Jessica wasn't too keen on watching anyone under eleven, but she did for Secret, because Secret always gave her big sisterly advice about boys.

Secret was putting on the finishing touches

of her make-up when Jessica rang the bell. "Open the door, Terrance. It's Jessica." After spraying her perfume, Secret pranced out the door. She gave the children a kiss and warned them to behave.

"You smell good, Mommy," Tika said as she gave her a hug. Secret winked and set sail on her mission. She drove five miles from her house and parked on a small side street near Uno's Restaurant. Secret hopped gracefully into the limo, parked on the opposite side of the street. A passionate kiss to the awaiting gentleman, and seconds later the driver was instructed to take off.

Chapter 12

Tarron was the last to arrive. The guys were on their second round of drinks, and the woman bashing had already begun. Tarron closed the door, and there was a pause in the conversation.

"Looka here, looka here," Ray said, breaking the silence. "The mack is in town."

"What up, fools?" Tarron smiled.

The guys all nodded except for Ray. Ray continued with, "Shit, nigga! I didn't know you were back in town."

"I got back the day before yesterday."

Jay wore an if-looks-could-kill expression.

"And you didn't have to holla back, to let a nigga know you weren't coming home." Ray laughed. "Don't I sound like the ol' ball and chain?"

"Wow, Ray, you sound like that man's wife, or at least his mistress, with the 'you can't call me' girl talk," Tweet chimed in. The other guys all laughed.

"Fuck you, man! Ain't that what I just said, nigga?" Ray slammed down his card.

"Naw, fuck you! You pretty motherfucka!"

"Both of you need to shut the hell up and get back to losing all of your hard-earned money to me," Jay shouted.

Tarron's and Kurt's laughter eased the tension that seemed to be building between Ray and Tweet. Tarron went straight past the card table and over to the bar to fix himself his usual Incredible Hulk. The guys were still laughing as he walked to his spot at the table.

"Hey, Tarron, you see Victoria this weekend?"

Tarron really didn't want to open up in front of his brother. "Damn, Ray, can I at least play one hand before we get into ho-house business?"

Three drinks and four hands later, Ray asked Tarron once again if he was ready to give up the scoop. Tarron threw his handful of small clubs and hearts on the table and told Ray to chill. *Now, this is the Ray that I have come to know and hate,* he thought as he got up from the table.

"Yaw niggas like some cackling women. Always want to know the scoop." Tarron laughed.

Tarron gave them a blow-by-blow account of what Victoria had set up for him. Jay was all ears. Tarron had a strong feeling that he should have held back on some of the information, but his boys got deep down into it. He got caught up in the moment. Once he put the period at the end of his story, he jetted to the bathroom.

Minutes later he strolled back, noticing Jay missing. Kurt and Tweet were playing Tunk, five dollars a hand.

"Where's Jay?" Tarron asked.

Kurt tightened his lips. "Jay got tired of playing with only three people and had a new hookup he knew was a sure thing, so he bounced." Tarron became instantaneously nervous.

Tweet and Kurt kept playing, while Ray and Tarron talked the business. In the back of his mind Tarron wondered who this new hookup was that Jay had to rush to. *He hasn't brought around any broads lately. That nigga's like sneaky Pete. He's up to his nose in something.*

"Hey, Tarron, did I tell you that I saw Secret

and Jay having lunch in Georgetown the other day?" Kurt blurted out.

Tarron gave Kurt a hard stare. "My Secret and Jay?"

"Yup, I was out picking up some supplies, and I walked past Houston's restaurant and saw them in there, having lunch. Man, I was distracted by this bad bitch with—"

"Man, just get to the point," Tarron huffed.

"Well, like I was saying. I looked up and saw them sitting at a table in the corner of the restaurant. I could see them, but they couldn't see me."

"You let that nigga leave outta here before letting me know?" Tarron bit his bottom lip. He paced the floor. He began mumbling under his breath; then came the loud out-burst.

"I'm sure it was nothing. Maybe they're planning something for your birthday," Kurt said.

"Planning . . . You think Jay is planning something? Fuck that!"

"How should I know? To be honest with you, I didn't think much of it, or else I would've called you on your cell that second."

Tarron was furious. He thought, *I wonder if Jay's new hookup is my wife.* He grabbed his jacket and rushed out the door.

"Yo, Tarron." Tweet tried to stop him. "What

the hell did you tell him that for?" Tweet could have knocked Kurt out.

"Why shouldn't I have told him? A man's wife . . . soon to be ex-wife"—he laughed—"can't have lunch with her brother-in-law?" Kurt was a prime candidate for the short bus.

"Would you want your wife to have lunch with your brother without you knowing if your brother was Jay?" Tweet argued.

"Damn, that nigga Jay is foul," Ray said. "I know Tarron feels like shit on a stick. Payback is a mother, but damn, not with your brother."

"This shows us all that what goes around comes right the hell back around," Tweet said.

"Makes me want to be on the straight and narrow." Ray poured himself another drink. "Say it ain't so. Say it ain't so."

"Yaw niggas act like something happened. Just chill." Tweet threw an empty beer can at Kurt.

Tarron raced down the Washington streets into Maryland. He left his briefcase on the front seat of the car and ran into the house. Secret was sitting in bed, reading *The Takeover* by Tonya Ridley, when Tarron came storming in.

"So, what did you do while I was out of town?"

"You ask me like you know already. What's got you so ticked?" she asked, placing her book on the bed.

"Why the hell were you and Jay having lunch together?"

"Me and who?"

Tarron got closer to the bed. "You and Jay," he repeated.

Secret pulled her legs out from under the covers and sat up on her knees. She could not seem to get comfortable in one position. Secret twitched like someone with Parkinson's disease. Small beads of sweat formed on her forehead as she tried to come up with the right words to say. Defensive, she said, "If you must know, we were talking about how you decided to back your friend Ray and not your blood brother, Jay, in the business."

"Girl, you know his past. I wouldn't have been able to find a company that would back any of his ideas," he replied as he sat down on the edge of the bed.

"That don't matter. You should have found somebody to help your brother."

Tarron stood. "Why the hell you so worried about Jay all of a sudden? What, you two fucking each other or something?" he shouted.

"You need to calm down. How dare you say

that to me. If I'm not mistaken, it was you that cheated on me in the past."

"Don't try and change the subject and put this on me," Tarron yelled.

"Put what on you?" she said with raised arms.

"Look, this is not going to work. I've already signed the lease for my new apartment!"

"Oh yeah! Well, tell that to your kids." Secret turned, pointing to Terrance and Tika, who were standing in the doorway.

Tarron's jaw dropped. Tika ran full speed ahead, diving into her dad's arms. "Daddy, don't go," Tika cried.

"We don't need you, anyway," Terrance said with conviction. "You ain't my daddy no more."

Tarron slowly peeled Tika from his leg. "Just fuck it. I'm outta here."

Chapter 13

When Tarron entered his office early that next morning, he felt revived. Shanice hadn't arrived, but she'd left a folder on his desk labeled IMPORTANT. Opening the folder, he stood dumbfounded. A huge red rejection stamp covered the title page. He scanned the next few pages of the proposal, wondering what could have gone wrong. He knew his personal life was starting to have an impact on his work; however, this was uncalled for. David knew his track record when it came to making the company money. *Why would he do something like this? Seems like nothing satisfies him these days.*

Tarron's emotions were already on edge from the night before. It had been days since his trip, and he still hadn't talked with Victoria. He didn't even tell her that he had moved out. With a slight touch of his mouse, he saw the message.

YOU'VE GOT MAIL.

He scanned the list of e-mails, but not one of them was from Victoria. He had to e-mail her immediately. He started typing away.

Victoria,

I miss you so much. I don't know what to do. Sitting at my office desk, I hear all of these songs playing on the radio that make me think of you. I want you!

It just doesn't even feel right with you so far away from me. I know that we can't spend that much time together. But it's just killing me being without you. A man in my state could be dangerous.

Sometimes it is hard just trying to imagine how it will be when we are finally able to be together out in the open. I can't wait.

You see, Victoria, when I think about you, I get a hard-on. When I hear your voice, I shake. What I'm about to say may seem strange and selfish, since I also have my problems, but here it goes.

Even though each time we spend together is special, it is never enough. I want you so much, and I'm becoming very impatient. I love you and I want to marry you. Still, you must understand and be willing to give me the things I need.

I need you to love only me. I need you to share your body with only me. I need you to care for me and make me feel like I'm the most important man in the world. I need you to be sincere, honest, and 100 percent real. Do you think you can handle all of this?

I would not ask these things of you if I did not feel I could do those things in return. I love you, Victoria, and I want only to make you happy.

He hit SEND.

Minutes later . . .

YOU'VE GOT MAIL.

Hey, Sweetie,

I'm so glad to hear from you. It really made me feel good. I was dying inside because I was trying not to e-mail you for a while. I felt you needed some time away from me to clear your head.

It seems you always know how to make me feel special, and reading your e-mail hit all the right spots. This one seemed to have a forever theme. I had no idea that you were becoming so confused about how you really felt when it came to us being together. I was not confused about how you feel about me, because I do know that you love me very much, but I'm trying to protect myself.

I was looking for any and every excuse to keep my feelings under control because of your wife. Then I read your e-mail and exploded. My heart rate increased, my pulse pounded, as fear raced up my spine. The fear of the unknown had overtaken me. You see, Tarron, we have something incredible going on right now. But will it be strong enough to last forever?

Sometimes, I think that the sneaking around helps fuel our burning desire for one another. But what will happen when our relationship becomes public and the spontaneity becomes routine? When seldom becomes daily and the simple becomes complex—what then?

Forever is a long time. Are we both looking at the same watch?

Tarron sat back in his chair. He took a long breath and immediately began to type his response.

Victoria,

It's funny that you make reference to time. I have spent years of my life with different women, and my emotional satisfaction from all those years can't compare to a few seconds of gratification I get when we are together.

No matter how much time passes by, I can't seem to get you out of my mind. The more I think about you, the more our first night comes to mind.

That night we connected, made time irrelevant, and turned casual sex into a love affair. The way you caressed my body and released your fears, I can still feel your juices dripping upon my lips.

That night was the turning point in my life. I had to realize that no one has ever made me feel the way you do—both mentally and physically. I need to know if I get under your skin bad enough that you feel you can't live without me, too.

He hit SEND.

YOU'VE GOT MAIL.

Tarron, my love,

Without you, I am like a butterfly without its wings, a heart without blood, and a body with no soul. It eases my pain to know that even though you are with another woman, it's me who you really love.

Although I am the other woman, I feel secure in our relationship. Plus, we have friendship coupled with loveship. And it's the friendship that will keep us together, no doubt.

The letters I receive in the mail with the "Would you be my lover on Friday?" and the homemade French toast with warm maple syrup waking me up after a night of incredible sex will keep me coming back for more, no matter what the situation.

I need for us to stay locked in this fairy-tale phase . . . the phase where everything is perfect when we are together. Oh yeah, the sex cannot change. . . .

You cater to my every want and need. You make me feel like the princess of the ball. And I often wish for the bell to never chime. You'll always have the match to my silver slipper.

Still, the biggest perk of all may be how you can express your feelings. It's your sensitivity I admire the most. When I read your e-mails, I am touched by the words you use. They make me wet.

You've got mail.

Peekaboo,
    Let's get together. . . .

Before he could finish typing, he was interrupted by an instant messenger. He saw it was Ray.

What up, fool?
    So how is your little place? I heard that you did a lot of bachelor shit. We should hold the next poker night at your spot instead of mine. You better be careful, because I just read in the *Washington Post* about this guy that got stabbed by his ex for cheatin', niggah. You better be careful! I think I saw Secret at the Amoco, filling up some containers full of gas. Watch it. Your crib might get burned to the ground.

                          Ha-ha-ha!
                          Ray

Tarron never responded. He wasn't in the mood for jokes. His attention was focused on two things, being a free man and starting a new life with Victoria.

Chapter 14

Tarron hooked up his little two-bedroom apartment and turned it into the bachelor's paradise he had always dreamed about. He hung out after work at the Lions' Den two or three times a week as well as Saturday nights. On the days he wasn't having drinks at the club and meeting new women, he was out with his children.

Victoria was now spending the entire night with Tarron on a regular basis. They were experiencing all the things that had eluded them when he was living at home with Secret. Long romantic walks along the Potomac River, pausing long enough to watch the planes take off or land at the airport across the water.

They met for lunch two or three times a week. She went grocery shopping with him, making sure he was buying food that was healthy. Some nights she ran his bathwater, she took him to the nail salon to get his hands and feet done, and she took him on getaways to exclusive bed-and-breakfast inns up and down the East Coast.

Although he wasn't officially divorced, and was out of his house only six months, Tarron was already sharing his new bachelor's pad with another woman. Sexy female clothing items decorated his bathroom shower door. There were tons of make-up products on the sink and alongside the tub. His oil-based abstract pictures of naked figures draped the walls of his bedroom. The array of colors allowed him the flexibility to choose any color scheme he desired.

All these changes were minor when compared to what he no longer had to endure. He was going to bed to the sounds of Luther and not screaming children. Either oral or some new form of bondage sex awoke him. He was the boss of his entire day. The children's schedule no longer dictated his whereabouts.

His newfound freedom did not interfere with his work. Even though he could stay out all night if he so decided, he never did. Even though he was now able to keep beer and alcohol in his refrigerator without fear that a child might try it, he never abused it. Even though he had his soul mate next to him every night, he was abusing this one item on the regular.

Sex was mandatory. It was like punching the clock at work. He could recall waking up some mornings believing that he had only dreamed he was having sex, to find himself naked and still dripping with the evidence that it was not just a dream.

The singles life quickly turned into the common-law marriage scenario. He really didn't mind, because Victoria gave him his space. Tarron never felt smothered by her. The constant nagging about bills, household dilemmas, his whereabouts, other women— and the list went on—no longer existed.

Victoria was even the one who reminded him about poker nights with the boys. Whenever he came home, she always had a home-cooked meal covered on the stove, and her warm, wet pussy waiting for him in between the sheets.

Victoria was no fool. She knew the things she had done to get him would be the same things she would have to do to keep him. She knew poker night with the boys had its benefits for her as well. Victoria could spend this time out with her girlfriends, doing her thing, or exploring her oats as well.

Time away from one another only built anticipation for the next time they met each other. Not only did being around others give them something different to talk about, it allowed their emotions to build. They say that absence makes the heart grow fonder, but it sure made for some incredible sex. Victoria knew that a night out drinking and talking about women with the boys would bring her tiger home, ready to devour his prey—her pussy.

Each hand of poker and power shot of booze would lead to more and more slut talk about women. Their stories of past conquests, lies about recent notches on their pistols, and comparisons of future fantasies would stir up all those bottled-up lustful desires, which she would be happy to help him uncork and release. The singles life was not everything he thought it would be. In some ways it was even better; in other ways it was much, much worse.

While Tarron lived the glamorous life, Secret suffered in silence. Her condition worsened by day. She knew she had the responsibility of maintaining the house but couldn't seem to pull herself together. Depression had gotten the best of her. Motherdear was forced to care for her and the children a few times during the week.

"I can't believe this house is so junky," Motherdear said on her initial visit, as she stepped over piles of cluttered clothes and toys thrown in the center of the kitchen floor. It had been days since she had talked with Secret. Like any dejected woman, Secret was not in the mood to return any calls. She turned the ringers off on every phone in the house.

Secret seldom spoke. She moved through the house like a spaced-out mummy. The children had total rein, like they owned the spot. She spent most of her time confined to her room. "Yes," was Secret's response to every question Tika and Terrance asked her. After a couple of weeks, the children were no longer concerned about their mother's condition, because they could do whatever they wanted. Their control lasted until Motherdear came on her regular Mondays, Fridays, and Sundays after church.

"Look now, Secret, I'ma need to cut at least one of them ringers on." Secret ignored

Motherdear. She marched over to Secret and gently lifted her chin.

"Okay, Motherdear. Have it your way," Secret said, shoving her hand away.

Motherdear, somewhat shocked, backed up and leaned against the wall. She rested her arms on her large breasts and continued her sermon. "You got to pull yourself together now, chile. Those children need their mother . . . and in her right mind. Now, you listen and listen good. Never let a man take you down to the point where you lose the desire to live. No man, as much as I love him, not even my own son, is worth all this pain you putting yourself through. See, men can leave you without your dignity and self-worth, but they move on with life. Chile, you gotta dig deep and pull yourself together. Just face it, phase two of your existence is waiting for you."

She threw herself on her pillow. "My life is over, Motherdear! I'm worthless."

Motherdear did not play into her pity party. "You sit with what I said. Just remember what the good Lord said . . . *and this, too, shall pass.*" Motherdear kissed Secret and walked out the door.

Hours later Secret felt some comfort from her mother-in-law's words. Motherdear tucked the children in and went home. As Secret got up to use the bathroom, the telephone rang. *I don't know why I let her turn on my ringer.* She ignored the sound and proceeded to the bathroom. Whoever was on the other end was persistent. When Secret wouldn't pick up, the person kept calling back. Finally, after about ten tries, she answered.

"What?" she said, impersonating a drunk.

"Hi, Secret. It's me, David."

"Mr. Jordan. It's been a while." Secret sat straight up in the middle of her mattress. "How are you?" She straightened her hair, as if he could see her.

"Look, I need to talk to you about something. This whole thing with Tarron is getting too sticky. And with me being his boss and all . . ."

"What the hell are you saying? Tarron left me, and now you!"

"No . . . just for now, let's chill." David waited for a response.

Secret said nothing.

"Don't sit and cry your pretty eyes out over Tarron," David said. "He's not worth it. Besides, he'll have a lot to cry about soon. I'll keep you posted."

"Sure." Secret hung up. She couldn't believe it. Tears streamed from her swollen eyes. She threw the cordless handset against the dresser and broke the mirror. Glass splattered everywhere. "Fuck you," she said, falling from the bed. Secret hit her head on the corner of Tarron's nightstand, and blood dripped from her temple. She hit the floor like a rag doll and didn't move.

Chapter 15

The first time Tarron had any real contact with Secret was when the judge ordered them to go to marriage counseling before he would grant their divorce. Tarron was sitting at the wooden, rectangular table with his lawyer when the courtroom doors opened. Slowly, Secret entered and effortlessly walked down the aisle. At first glance, he thought she resembled a crackhead. Secret's weight had dropped considerably. Her eyes had swelled like she'd been in a brawl. Her hair was unkempt, and her once glowing complexion dry. *Why the gauze on her head?*

Damn, she going down. Tarron couldn't believe this was the same woman he married. She looked nothing like the queen he'd come to

know on that faithful day. He thought back to
their wedding.

Everyone was standing and admiring how
stunning she was as she strutted with her father in Greater Hope Baptist Church. The
two-carat diamond choker around her neck
sparkled with every step. It took three of
Tarron's little nephews to follow behind her
and hold the ends of her enormous train,
making sure it didn't get caught on anything.

Their wedding was huge. Twenty members
in the wedding party alone—over five hundred friends and family in attendance. Seventy-
five white doves were spread around the
church and then released at the reception.
There were so many gifts that they had to continue opening them after they returned from
their honeymoon.

Tarron snapped back to reality when the
wooden gate closed behind Secret with a bang
as she sat next to her lawyer. Tarron wasn't trying to stick it to Secret or cheat her in any way,
because part of him still loved her. The judge
could sense this in many of Tarron's answers,
and he could also tell that she loved him, too,
despite her confused state of mind.

"I don't feel that you two are good candi-
dates for divorce. You have children, and you
seem to really have a lot of unresolved emotions. My theory is that you call it quits when

each of you has utilized every tool. Try outside help to clear up some of your little cloudy barriers. I am going to order you both into marriage counseling, and if at that time I get the news that this marriage is at the point of divorce, I will grant this request. Court's adjourned," the judge shouted with a bang of his gavel.

Dr. Sharone Robinson was a highly esteemed family therapist in the area and was given the case of *Jenkins v. Jenkins*. She specialized in marriage therapy for young black couples with children. The first session was devoted to exploring why their relationship declined. When they became acquainted with Dr. Robinson, she positioned them both in oversized burgundy leather chairs only feet apart from one another.

"How did you two meet?" Dr. Robinson gnawed on the arm of her eyeglasses.

At the same time both of them began to answer. "At a party . . ." Then Tarron stopped to allow Secret to finish.

Dr. Robinson asked several more general questions, which they took turns answering.

"How did you end up here?"

Tarron looked over at Secret. Secret looked back at him.

"We are here because my husband of so many years believes that his mistress is his soul mate, and he chose his soul mate over our marriage, our children, and our life."

Tarron rubbed his hands over his face and turned to Dr. Robinson. He was thinking to himself that Secret had summed up their life, his second life, and their dilemma in one simple statement that took up only a minute. The buzzer sounded on the small clock on Dr. Robinson's desk, and their first session was over. Dr. Robinson worked out the date of their next session and gave them both a professional handshake.

The first two weeks of therapy were basic. Upon their return, the sessions became more in depth.

"Doc, my childhood has very little to do with these feelings that I am experiencing," Tarron said.

"But, Tarron, how do you really feel about this whole ordeal?"

"It's not just about me. Why don't you ask Secret any questions?"

"Secret, how is this ordeal affecting you?"

"This is crazy. I really can't understand why any of this is happening."

The doctor asked Secret if she had ever been aware of her husband cheating prior to him leaving.

"I had my reservations. Our sex life had deteriorated immensely, though when it was good, it was great." She looked at Tarron. "With the exception of one incident of infidelity years ago, I trusted my man. But now, in hindsight, I feel like such a fool. I see everything he told me about working late and his business trips were probably just lies. I never saw the signs."

The therapist wrote as Secret talked. She periodically glanced over her glasses to make note of the body language of each.

Secret went on to say, "We never had any real fights in all our years of marriage. He gave in to every disagreement we had about any issue. But I guess so, since he had a play toy on the side all along. Tarron was an excellent father, but I question his ability to be an effective husband."

"I was a good husband," Tarron shouted. "I tried to keep my affair with her in the closet. I never flaunted her in the open. Nor did I allow it to interfere with you and the kids." He looked at Secret.

"It was a relationship of chance. We just seemed to be in the same place at the same time. My nights out and scheduled business trips were just that. She was involved in some aspect of the deal I was working on, so we would be in that same place at the right time.

Me and Victoria began only because I wanted and needed to do things, sexual things that I didn't want to do with my wife. Look, Doc, no disrespect, but I like wild sex and my wife doesn't. That's not why I married her. She definitely serves her purpose."

Secret's mouth dropped wide open. "A slave?" she yelled out. "And what the fu . . . What's so special about this home wrecker? What does she look like, huh, Tarron? Is she that damn fine?" Secret was prepared to kick his ass. "Oh, sorry, Doc, but I can't believe this mother . . ." Secret bit her lip. Tears dripped in her lap.

She'd broken the number one rule: *only one person speaks at a time.* The only privilege the listener had was to take notes. Dr. Robinson understood the reason for her outburst but reminded her of the rule.

So Secret dried her face and put an extra grip on her pen and jotted on her paper. "Oh, so you see me as a slave. Tell that bitch V-i-c-t-o-r-i-a to throw on the damn scarf and apron."

Tarron put himself in the deep end of the sin. It was all or nothing. He continued. "I like to do wild sexual things, pseudomasochism, threesomes, you know, the works. I need spice, variety. . . ."

"I get the picture," the therapist assured.

"These aren't things I wanted to do or even

could see doing with Secret. She is the mother of my kids. She kisses them to sleep at night. I just wanted some freaking nasty shit like the old days. I compromised a lot when I got married to Secret. Still, some things I hoped she'd compromise on once we got married. But that didn't happen." Tarron's facial expression showed that he was frustrated. "Take her attitude on anal sex. My penis better not even brush against it during position changes, or the mood was lost."

That's what you think, Secret thought. As she reflected back on that day, an unusual smile came over her face, which caused both Tarron and Dr. Robinson to pause.

"I love my wife. I will always love my wife. I just wanted to let the Mandingo out and be a warrior sometimes."

Tarron surrendered his time for comments from Dr. Robinson. "Secret, would you like to respond to your husband's comments?"

Secret's anger prevented her from being able to speak.

"Well, I think a lot of things were shared, and we will continue this in two weeks, when I return from my conference. Thank you both for coming, participating, and respecting one another. See you in two weeks."

Secret knocked Tarron over leaving the office. Picking himself up from the leather couch, he waited for Dr. Robinson to say something. She didn't. He caught up with Secret in front of the elevators.

"When I find out who she is, that whore is dead. And as for you, Mr. Long Dick, I hope you catch a disease and the shit falls off in your hand." She clenched her fist tight.

When the elevator doors opened, he let her get on alone. Tarron dared not get on the same elevator with her. She'd turned into a beast.

"You're gonna regret you ever met me!" The doors closed.

Chapter 16

Tarron's attitude was blown. After the episode with Secret, he couldn't focus on anything but her threats. *Would she really do something physical to hurt me or my woman?* Reluctant to open his e-mail messages, Tarron clicked on the one titled "Me Again."

Black man,
 I hope this note finds you picking your black ass off the ground piece by piece. A little birdie told me you moved out. It's about fuckin' time. That beautiful woman doesn't need you or your bullshit. I don't even think you ever loved her. And what's up with the head shrink? That's right. My birdie told me everything. I know somebody with a magic

stick you can use to talk. And the stick is a whole lot bigger than the one your mother circumcised. Instead of that "you didn't hold me enough shit," maybe you need to **ASK SECRET TO SHARE HER SECRET ABOUT THE NIGHT YOU GUYS MET.** Real problems call for real solutions. The head shrink will earn her pay then. Her mommy didn't name her Secret because the name sounded good. She's got some *secrets* for your ass. Your entire marriage was a fake. You thought you got her, but she got you. And in more ways than one.

Tarron must have read that e-mail a hundred times before printing a copy to take with him to the next counseling meeting. The line "Ask Secret to share her *secret* about the night you guys met" took up residence in his head. The author had placed that line in large black capital letters. This anonymous person knew a great deal, but their language was no clear giveaway. He studied each sentence, looking for any clue that would reveal the identity of the instigator. No such luck. The more he read, the more frustrated he became. Who knew about Dr. Robinson? Who knew about the night they met? Who knew all these things but was too afraid to show themselves? Secret had to be the one talking, because he hadn't spoken a word to anyone, he thought, not even Victoria.

Finally, he clicked the mouse to return to his list of more recent e-mails. Some of them were from different business clients; others were junk mail from telemarketers. As he scrolled farther down the screen, he noticed an e-mail from Secret. It was titled "Children." He clicked on the message.

Tarron,
I hate you, you bastard! How many times have you really messed around on me? You messed up our life. The times I thought were good . . . not! Yeah, your pile of skeletons fell from the closet, but guess what, Mr. Jenkins? You punk, what would you have done without me? I got some bones of my own . . . big-ass brontosaurus bones.

Damn, I loved you, Tarron . . . more than life itself. Why you do me like this? You were my forever. I put everything into you and the kids. I can't take this no more. These dark moments are way too much for me to bear.

You coward! I would clean between your dirty-ass toes if you asked me to. So what, I wasn't the freak you desired?

How the hell you think you'll turn a ho
into a damn housewife? Ooh, I hate you,
but I still love you. Can't you understand
my pain?
            The One Who Put Up With Yo Shit!

Secret needs to be admitted into the psych ward,
Tarron thought. *I'd better watch my back.*

Victoria reminded Tarron that it was the
third Thursday of the month.

"I don't think I'm going."

"Baby, you gotta get out of this house," she
said.

"Look, after what happened to me these
past two days, I don't know if I can stand seeing my brother, Jay."

"Tarron, you have to face him one day. He's
the younger brother, so why are you running?
You need a good laugh. Go on out so you and
the boys can talk about big tits and whatever
else."

Tarron began to smile. Victoria made sense
in her not-so-funny way. He knew she needed
a break from him sulking around the house
every night. Tarron grabbed his hat and
jacket and headed for the door. Victoria followed him, sending him off with a juicy kiss.

* * *

Tarron stood out in front of Tweet's apartment, trying to put names to the voices he heard coming from inside. Finally he knocked. Tweet opened the door.

"Shit, it's about damn time," Tweet said as he held out his fist. Tarron gave him a pound and chest bump.

"Nigga, you know where I live."

From the other side of the apartment, Ray and Kurt yelled, "Tee," reminiscent of that old show *Cheers*.

Tarron gave them some dap, a few pats on the back, and settled into his chair.

"Come on, let's play some cards. Daddy needs a new pair of shoes," Tarron said, laughing.

As soon as Ray dealt the first hand, there was a knock at the door. Tarron swallowed as Tweet jogged to get it. He thought it was Jay. When he heard Tweet ask how much, Tarron sighed a big sigh of relief. *It's not Jay, just the deliveryman,* he thought.

When Tarron turned his head toward the door, three thick, beautiful, sexy dancers were entering the apartment. Tarron had seen them dance at the club before, so he was well aware of their skills. The fun was about to begin.

"You been down for too many days now. What better way to cheer you up than to treat you to these fine-ass tricks? Watch these chicks turn some tricks. The hot-to-def bodies will make you forget every problem you ever had," Ray hollered as the girls circled Tarron. The boys rooted.

Candy Cane was the first to dance. She pushed Tarron in a dining room chair centered in the middle of the floor. Ray blasted Ready for the World's song "Tonight." Candy Cane straddled Tarron, teasing him with her grapefruit-sized breasts. She made him bite the strawberry caught between. She took off her red and white thong and massaged Tarron's penis with her undergarment.

Cameo's "Candy" played in the background. Without missing a beat, she began to pull a string of beads out of her pussy and looped them around her neck. Tarron sat in amazement as she slowly continued to pull the eight-inch string of red and white beads during the entire record. She kneeled to kiss his penis when the song was over.

Kitty Kat's routine was faster paced. Tarron's eyes bounced up and down, trying to keep up with the Jell-O jiggle of her immense buttocks. She rolled over on her back, pulled her legs over her head, and made the lips of her pussy ripple to the music. Kitty Kat gave Tarron a thick, nine-inch glass dildo and swung her right leg up onto his shoulder. Tarron was now in a face-to-face position with her dripping treasure. He began to play with her clit, using the dildo. As Kitty Kat leaned back to touch the floor with her hands, Tarron inserted the whole nine inches into her. His boys got hard. She came.

Trixie got her name because her routine dealt more with tricks and props than actual dance moves. Her first trick was picking up a four-ounce bottle with her vagina and filling it to the top with thick womanly fluids. She then picked up two large strawberries from a bowl and placed them in Ray's mouth. She did this while Ray got down on his knees. Her last trick was nothing short of amazing. Trixie had a twelve-inch-long dildo that needed kickstands to hold it up. She had to step on a small footstool to position herself over the dildo. Then slowly, she lowered her wanting body over the head and took in the entire dildo.

Tarron thought it might be one of those collapsible toys. But when she finished and he tried to push it down, it didn't budge. He could feel her juices covering every inch of the dildo. Trixie lifted herself and danced by

Tarron's side. She placed his hand in her hole. Trixie raked his fingers, dripping with juice, across her lips.

Tarron was so worked up, he rushed to get home. When he turned the key, Victoria was lying naked on the couch, ready and waiting.

"I knew those girls would send you home in the right frame of mind."

"You set that up?"

"Of course. I knew you could use a little male fun. I had to get you out of that funk, baby. You've been neglecting *Mommy*. Now, get over here, so I can ride you like Trixie rode that big thang."

Tarron couldn't undress fast enough. He tripped over his pants trying to come out of them. Victoria lay there, warming up her machine. She massaged between her lips until all the dryness disappeared. Watching his bulging penis made her temperature rise. Tarron directed her onto her stomach. He stumbled toward Victoria like a one-year-old. No need for the baby oil. He didn't even touch her vagina. "Keep your finger there," he said, going straight for her second hole. Tarron attempted to slide his shaft directly in.

Victoria didn't mind taking it in the ass, but never dry and never in the beginning of sex. She was relieved when it missed the entry point and slid farther back out from between her legs.

Tarron got the hint. He lifted her from the couch and carried her to the bedroom. After laying her on the bed, Tarron reached for the baby oil and squirted a long stream of it on each leg. Using both hands, he rubbed her thighs, her calves, and her feet. Grabbing her hips firmly, he rolled her back over.

He handcuffed both her wrists to the metal headboard with her cuffy-cuffs. He left the bed and returned moments later with three neckties from the closet.

He tied her ankles to the bottom bedposts. Now Victoria lay spread eagle between the four corners of the queen-size bed. He left again to get his blindfold out of his sock drawer.

Victoria was totally helpless and at the mercy of Tarron. She began to ask questions. So many that he pushed a washcloth into her mouth and tied it with the third necktie. She could only grunt and shake her head from left to right and right to left.

Tarron began by dripping hot candle wax onto her naked chest. He was trying desperately to spell his name with it. Victoria flinched as the hot wax made contact with her skin. The seconds of pain from each drop were jump-starting her pussy juices once again.

Tarron decided she wasn't ready yet. He whispered, "I'll be back," into her ear. She could hear his faint footsteps as he walked out of the room. So many thoughts ran through her mind as she lay there in complete darkness, unable to move.

Anticipation turned to fear, because it was taking Tarron a really long time to return. But when he did, he watched her body twist as she fought to remove the cuffs from her wrists. The muscles in her legs tightened as she attempted to rip the silk ties.

Freezing drops of water caused her body to tremble. Tarron knew she loved ice cubes. It wouldn't take long for him to erase the fear and start her juices flowing again. He bit off a piece of ice and started to suck her nipples, using his tongue to press the ice against them. The harder he sucked, the more her back arched.

Her body squirted out globs of liquid as her back relaxed. Tarron slid his tongue down the center of her body, chasing an escaping ice cube. He slid the ice through her pussy fast but allowed his tongue to follow slowly. Nibbling on her lips made her back rise again.

Teardrops ran down her cheeks from under

the blindfold. Another orgasm was near. This time, she squirted with even more force. Cum splashed against Tarron's tonsils. He flung himself on top of her and shoved his throbbing penis into her.

Finally, the foreplay was over, and her entire pussy experienced his pleasure. Her walls held on like a vise grip as he pushed deeper into her. Using the metal bars from the headboard, he pushed his entire shaft and the head of his balls into her.

The washcloth in her mouth became saturated. She shook the bed as she pulled and tugged to free her limbs.

Tarron pulled out his vibrating bullet and slid it along her breast. The bullet felt good to both of them. Tarron removed the cloth from her mouth and slid his penis over her lips. She licked the tip, and he reached down below to untie her legs. Tarron clutched her ankles and pulled her legs up until her butt was high in the air.

He straddled her. This position caused a tremendous amount of pressure on her neck, but she knew Tarron was aware of this. He called this his upside-down doggy style. He loved this position because his downward motion allowed him the fun of smacking her ass.

Tarron stayed in the upside-down doggy

style a little longer this time. Victoria had to kick out her legs and bend his dick the wrong way in order to get him to stop.

She was mad. Not mad, mad, but mad. When Tarron made the mistake of releasing her arms from their restraints, she tackled him and handcuffed him facedown to the headboard.

She ran to the closet and snatched out one of Tarron's leather belts. She used both hands to make the belt make that popping sound as she walked back to the bed.

The alpha lash caught Tarron by surprise. Victoria was swinging with great force. The belt left a raised red mark across his ass. Tarron began to kick at Victoria, shouting, "Girl, you better not hit me that hard again."

"Bone up. Be a man. You took more when you pledged."

"I ain't playing. Don't hit me so hard."

"Make a choice, then, crybaby!"

"Between what?"

"More smacks with this belt or my dildo in your ass."

"Neither."

Tarron pulled so hard on the cuffy-cuffs that the headboard pounded the wall. *Kapow!* The belt crackled against his ass again. Tarron was fired up. He jerked each arm and popped the metal links. He grabbed Victoria and slammed her on the bed face-first.

"So, you thought that was funny," he said as he pressed his weight down on her. He spread her legs with his legs. In one swift motion, he jammed his dick into her ass. Victoria let out a great scream.

He twirled her hair around his hand and yanked her head back.

"You want things in butt holes, huh?"

"Is that all you got? Bone up."

Tarron began to pound his dick deeper into her ass. Never pausing, he pounded her ass until both of them could take no more. They lay there in silence. Neither of them said a word or touched each other.

Chapter 17

Tarron was eager to get to work that morning, but his body was feeling the aftermath of Victoria's sex marathon. He got the company to send over a driver to pick him up.

When he entered the building, everyone seemed extra nice that morning. It could have been his imagination, but they were all so glad to see him. *Maybe it's my Victoria's secret glow that's got them going.* Tarron shook more hands than usual. When he got to his office, Shanice greeted him in the same manner.

"Good morning, Mr. Jenkins."

"Shanice, it's nice to see you."

"Is there anything I can get for you, sir . . . orange juice, apple juice, maybe some hot tea?"

"No thank you, Shanice. I'm fine."

Shanice opened the door to his office and closed it behind him. Tarron stood there for a minute, scanning his office. He took a deep breath and thought, *It's great to be in the land of the living*.

Tarron headed straight for his computer. One click of the mouse and the words were music to his ears. Nothing could upset his day, that day.

YOU'VE GOT MAIL.

Tarron searched through the many e-mails that had been sent and saw an address that caught his eye. It was between an e-mail from David and a "Big Butts in Cancún" flyer from Tweet. It was titled "Secret *Secrets*."

He clicked on the e-mail.

Poor little man. You think that you've done something by moving out. It was wrong to stay, knowing you were cheating, but it's even more wrong to leave your wife and children for your mistress. You need to find yourself. You will never be happy until you realize who you are and what you really want.

He clicked again.

Tarron went back to the long list of unread e-mails and scrolled down until he came to another e-mail from an anonymous author.

The news on the grapevine is that you and your wife are finally starting to talk about some real issues at counseling. Brace yourself, young brother. You ain't uncovered nothing yet. People always start by painting half the picture. By the end of your session, expect the bomb to drop. You have only begun your journey to total awareness. The new answers you find are only found in the blood. Remember that blood is thicker than water.

He clicked out of the e-mail.

Tarron was lost. The little notes were making no sense to him. *Answers are found only in the blood. What is that supposed to mean? What is the reference to new answers? What questions do I still seek? I'm straight.* Tarron glimpsed at his watch and realized he was going to be late for his therapy session with his court-appointed shrink.

Dr. Robinson could tell that something was different with Tarron from the very beginning of the session. He was very short with all his answers and watched more than he participated.

The session moved slowly at first. Dr. Robinson suggested they both participate in her new breathing techniques. When time was up, Tarron quickly spoke without Dr. Robinson's permission.

"I have been receiving e-mails from a person who won't identify him- or herself. The e-mails are detailed, and they discuss things that are very personal. No other person should know about this session, unless somebody has been running their fuckin' mouth." He slammed the copy of the printed e-mail message on the table.

"Tarron, please remember the rule that prohibits the use of foul language. Cursing automatically causes a person to become defensive."

"Sorry, Dr. Rob, but these e-mails are really touching home. I can take her crazy ass sending me schizophrenic e-mails, but when people start to make references about my past personal business, I lose it. They even talked as if they knew more about me and the dealings of my life than I do."

Secret sat listening attentively to Tarron talk. She uncrossed her legs and switched them as she crossed them again.

"This person has the nerve to even give me advice on how I should proceed in therapy with my head shrink. No offense, Doc."

"None taken."

"That's just how they referred to you in the last e-mail."

Secret reached down with her right hand to rub her calf.

"Am I boring you, Secret? I mean, you are doing a whole lot of moving. Plus, I don't see you taking any notes on this session. Is it because you know something?"

"You sound like you're paranoid," she replied.

"Paranoid? Huh! Tell me why they directed me to ask you to let out your secret about the night we met."

Tarron searched Secret for answers. She hesitated before speaking. Secret took a sip from her glass of water and then looked directly at Tarron.

"That night at the Touchdown Club was a long time ago. It started when my girlfriend Alexis talked me into going to this party she heard about. We were sitting in my living room, drinking, and at the last minute decided to go."

She adjusted herself in her chair and continued. "We didn't know anyone at the club, so we settled in a booth, drank a little more, and watched the people. To make the night more exciting, we started a little game of Truth or Dare." The more Secret spoke, the angrier she became. Her erratic mood swings concerned the therapist. Secret's voice became elevated. "We played that a lot, but when it was just the girls, more *truth* questions were asked. But with so many guys around, it was *dare's* turn to rule."

She twisted the bottom of her blouse. Secret regretted having to relive the events all over again. "It started off minor. You know, I dare you to dance with that guy. I dare you to squeeze that guy's butt. But as the night went on, they got deeper and wilder."

Secret turned to look in another direction. "I dare you to French-kiss that guy. I dare you to stroke that guy's penis. I dare you to suck that guy off in the bathroom. I dare you to fuck that guy outside. That was my dare."

"What?" Tarron shouted.

"I was buzzing from liquor, and the guy they chose was sexy and had it going on. I really wasn't thinking. It was the third time I'd had sex on the first date, so it wasn't a big deal. You know when you're young, you do crazy acts like that. I walked up to him and asked if he could help me to my car. When he said yes, we walked outside. As we ambled to the car, I told him some bullshit about him being the sexiest man I had ever seen and that I wanted to fuck the shit out of him right there." Secret took a deep breath.

"We walked around the corner and found a deep, dark entryway to some office building. I gave him a rubber and we did it. It didn't last long, nor did he rock my world. It must have been the position, because the rubber popped. I didn't find out about this until later.

"Anyway, I came back into the club. We had a few laughs and discussed the dare. We then decided to take a picture. That's when you came over to me with that lame-ass line about a picture, but I found you to be everything that I told that stranger."

Tarron's pupils dilated continuously in his head as Secret's bones fell out one by one.

"I called you the very next day, and we had sex every day for the next two weeks. It wasn't until he came home from prison that I realized the guy from the club was your brother."

Tarron exploded out of his chair. The force sent the chair clear across the room. Dr. Robinson jumped up, as if to run out of her office. Secret didn't flinch.

"My fuckin' brother! And you fuckin' chewin' me out about sleeping around?"

Secret paused as she got a tighter grip on

her chair. Her intentions were to smack the shit out of Tarron if he got simple in that office.

"It was Jay."

"You fucked my little brother and never told me."

Tarron hastened back and forth. Finally, he stopped and laughed like a psychotic madman. *Karma, that's what it is. I'm getting paid back for all the times I was unfaithful to you. It's like I broke the law years ago, and now the fine is just catching up with me. It's time to pay the piper, that's all. My brother . . . my wife . . . This is some real heavyweight bullshit. Damn, look how she was so smooth about hers. A woman never changes her routine. That's what my father always told me.*

Tarron just went over and picked up his chair and apologized for his outburst. Dr. Robinson sat down and began writing like a slave running for freedom.

"Why didn't you tell me?" Tarron acted normal again.

"Your brother went to jail the next day, remember? I didn't see him again until he came home eight years later. At first I didn't even recognize him. We had already been married several years. When he finally realized who I was, we both decided that there wasn't any reason to tell you, because it was nothing. The short fling we'd had was no competition to our union. Why damage our marriage? It was just a dare, and I didn't think I would ever see him again. Nor did I ever think that he could be my future brother-in-law."

Dr. Robinson continued to jot down notes. Tarron wanted to speak. Secret pushed back in her chair.

"You and my little brother, my never-do-right brother, my ex-con brother, and you made a decision about what would be best for me. Then you two lived more years keeping this incident a secret in order to protect my feelings and our marriage. I guess I shouldn't be upset. I should be thankful you and my brother fucked and kept it a secret for years. Now I understand, Secret. The facts of our entire marriage have been a secret to me. I don't know you, and you definitely don't know me."

Tarron stood up and slammed his fist on the desk. He hastily paced to the door. As he rotated the knob, he looked back and said, "It was nice to meet you, Doc, but you'll never see me again."

Tarron slammed the door as he walked out. Secret sobbed profusely. Dr. Robinson walked over to Secret and handed her a tissue.

"I fucked up, Dr. Robinson."

"Honey, I know it seems terrible right now, but remember it's always darkest before dawn."

"No, Doc. I don't think you understand what I'm saying. Jay and I fucking is only a small fraction of this burnt pie, and when Tarron finds out the inner layers under the black crust, he's going to kill me."

"Baby, he's not going to kill you. It's not that bad. Whatever it is, everything is going to be all right. Whether you are with or without Tarron, you're going to be fine."

While Secret openly shared the rest of the ingredients of her nasty poach with Dr. Robinson, Tarron was trying to reach Jay by cell, but he kept getting his voice mail. Tarron decided to call Ray to help calm him. He told him to meet him down at the club. Tarron was on his third drink, and Ray was downing his first.

"So, Tee, what's going on, man?"

"Let me ask you a question. If you and Secret had sex before I met her, and you didn't realize she was that girl until after we got married, would you tell me?"

"Of course I would."

"Then why wouldn't Jay tell me?"

"Jay had sex with Secret?"

"Yeah."

"Get the fuck out of here. You're joking, right."

"I wish I was."

"Damn, this calls for another round."

"Make it a double."

The girls started to arrive to work. Ray and Tarron were near being hammered. Tarron didn't feel like hanging around a bunch of people asking him what was wrong, so he decided to drive home and cuddle with Victoria.

Tarron stumbled out of the office and headed for the steps. He reached out for the rail but missed. He almost fell down the metal steps but caught his balance. Slowly he made his way down the steps. Just before he hit the fourth step, he came crashing down the last three steps. His head banged against the wall before coming to a halt on the plush carpet at the bottom.

Ray ran out of the office when he heard all the commotion. He ran to the steps to find Tarron picking himself up from the floor.

"Tarron, are you all right?" he shouted, scampering down the steps.

"Hell yeah, I'm fine. I just need to get home," Tarron said as he began to dust off his clothes.

"Are you sure that you can drive home? I can get one of the girls to take you," Ray said.

"I can drive home. The steps were just slippery. I think someone spilled their drink. You need to have someone clean them before you have a lawsuit," he replied, slurring his words.

Tarron stumbled to his car. He paused to rub his face with his hands in an attempt to clear the buzzing sound out of his head. The ignition revved out of control once he weighed down on the key too long. *I can do this.* Tarron put his BMW in drive and uncontrollably coasted down the main street. For an overly intoxicated man, he actually obeyed all the traffic light laws. Tarron stopped on red and proceeded on green. He did manage to take short naps in between rest stops.

Tarron managed enough strength to find the button to his window. The night air saved him, or so he thought. Tarron blasted the radio as loud as the law allowed in order to stay alert.

"Aw hell, all this talk about cheating relationships is making me sick." Tarron had had enough. Somehow, he figured he could put in one of his CDs. Tarron wrestled with the middle compartment to grab some real music. As he looked down, a car behind him beeped because the light had turned green. Tarron flagged the impatient driver and continued to retrieve his CD.

Five minutes passed, and Tarron was still

rummaging through his collections. "Teddy P., Luther, Jay-Z. That's it." He slipped the CD in the player after missing several times. Cars continued to go around him, assuming he had broken down. Tarron pressed his foot on the accelerator. After coasting through that intersection, a half a mile down he came to another light but this time was unable to brake. As he cruised through the red light, the unthinkable happened. Tarron was side-swiped by a FedEx delivery truck. The last thing he remembered was the bright lights.

Minutes later, people gathered as if they had paid to see a sideshow. The small fire developing underneath Tarron's car caused one of the bystanders to grab him from the wreck. His BMW had smashed into the sidewall of a 7-Eleven convenience store. The FedEx truck had hit a light pole and turned upside down.

After Tarron was pulled from his car, another man rushed to get something to stop the blood from gushing out of Tarron's head. The Good Samaritan ripped off his shirt and applied pressure to his wound.

"Can you talk?" he yelled in Tarron's ear three times.

Tarron groaned. He made several attempts to move his fingers. Flashing lights made him panic.

"No, don't move. Help is on the way," the

man said. "Over here. He's losing a lot of blood," he yelled to the medical team. The bald-headed man waved in their direction.

The paramedics took over like he was dying. They removed the makeshift bandage and gave his wound appropriate medical attention. Tarron was in serious condition.

Chapter 18

Tarron strained through his engorged eyes to see around the room. The extreme weight of the casts on his left arm and leg made it difficult for him to move. His body felt like someone had stabbed needles through it. Tarron got nervous when he tried to move and the large machine beside his bed beeped.

Off to his right, he saw Victoria sleeping in a knot on a lounge chair. She seemed uncomfortable. He called out her name, but no sound parted his lips. His attempts to speak woke Victoria.

"Oh, baby, I'm so glad you've come back to me."

His ashy mouth didn't change how she felt about kissing him. Victoria knelt down and smooched him across the lips. He made what appeared to be a smile. She didn't need to hear his voice; she was glad to see him conscious. She quickly poured him a glass of water and tried to bring his bed upright so that he could drink.

Accidentally, she pushed the wrong button. The bed came crashing down flat, causing him tremendous pain. Tarron grunted in agony.

The door flew open and Secret entered. She had heard Tarron's cries.

"Oh, hell no!" As Secret moved closer, she recognized Victoria. *I know this ain't the same wench who was at my son's birthday party . . . up in my damn house!*

"Bitch, I promised to kill your ass when I ran into you. You had the nerve to come be in my house, eatin' my damn food, puttin' your nasty ass on my toilet seat? I ought to put you next to his sorry ass!" Secret yelled.

Victoria paid Secret no mind, continuing to restore the bed to a comfortable position for her man.

"Slut, did you hear me? Get your fuckin' hands off my husband."

"Your husband?" Victoria took a stand.

"Yes, my husband. I am Mrs. Jenkins, his wife of five years."

"Save that shit for someone who doesn't

know you. He ain't sleeping with you every night. Let me check the record. . . . Um, he moved out of your house months ago. So, bitch, you back the fuck up."

That comment did it. Secret leaped, landing a right hook across Victoria's jawbone. Secret held tightly to Victoria's shirt as Victoria dropped to the floor. Secret, straddled over the bottom of Tarron's bed, continued to throw blows to Victoria's face. At the same time, Secret reached for her hair, pulled a chunk from her scalp. Although she was a grown woman, she had no reservations about fighting like she was back in high school.

Tarron watched the entire scene as if it were a pay-per-view boxing match. All he could do was moan. He felt sorry that he could do nothing to help his mistress. Secret took it to her. As soon as Victoria was able to get loose from Secret, she stumbled out of the door yelling for help.

Several nurses came running from behind the nurses' station. The Spanish nurse picked Victoria up from the floor, helped her back into the room. Everything had happened so quickly, no one had heard the commotion. They entered the room and looked at Secret.

"Excuse me, miss. Who are you, and what are you doing here?" an obese nurse asked.

"This is my damn husband, and that bitch

right there is his mistress. Ask that ho to present some ID," Secret huffed, ready to charge again.

"I'm sorry, miss. Only immediate family members are allowed to visit at this time. You must show identification, or I'm going to have to ask you to leave," the head nurse said to Victoria.

"And, bitch, you are none of the above," Secret said sarcastically.

"Look, Mrs. Jenkins, I'm going to have to ask you to lower your voice. This is a hospital."

"Bitch, I know you didn't just call me a bitch," Victoria said, looking through her purse.

"If it walks like a female dog, talks like a female dog, and goes in heat like a female dog, it must be a bitch. Now, present some ID, heffa."

"I've got your heffa."

Victoria came running around the bed just as a security guard stepped into the room in front of Secret. He caught the full power of Victoria's right hook. He stumbled back, then grabbed hold of Victoria before she could swing again.

"You done messed up now, bitch." Secret laughed.

Victoria tried to get out of the security guard's arms but couldn't. She even tried to kick Secret as he pulled her into the hallway. The head nurse was raising the bed when she decided that Secret had to leave as well.

"This is my husband, and I'm not going anywhere!"

"If this is your husband, you will still have to step out until I get him stable. And I need to see some ID!"

"I'll step outside, but I'm not leaving."

Secret walked out into the hallway and saw the security guard talking with Victoria at the nurses' station. She waved bye-bye to Victoria, and once again, the guard had to restrain her.

"Look, you are going to have to calm down, before I call the police to arrest you for disorderly conduct," said the guard as he held on tighter.

"I'm leaving! Let me go. I said I'm leaving, but, Secret, you better believe that I'll be back."

Secret used her cell phone to call her girlfriends and Motherdear. When Victoria arrived at the hospital the next morning, she found out that Tarron's mother had instructed the nurses not to let her in.

Victoria was arguing loudly in the hall when they told her that she couldn't see Tarron. Secret stepped out of the room when she heard all the yelling. With this smug smile on her face, she waved bye-bye once again to Victoria.

Victoria started to walk toward Secret. Secret's friends all stepped out from the visitors' waiting room and surrounded Victoria. Victoria was upset, and four against one wasn't going to stop her from getting one lick in on Secret.

Motherdear came around the corner from getting some coffee and saw Victoria in the middle of Secret and her friends with her fist clenched.

"Victoria," she shouted.

"Mother Jenkins," she responded.

"Baby, I know you love my son, but this is not the time or place for what you are thinking."

Victoria stood there looking at Mrs. Jenkins.

Motherdear realized that Secret was watching her also.

"Motherdear, you know her, too?" Secret shouted. "So, I'm the last to know!"

Victoria smirked. "That's not all, wifey. Check the dent in your bathroom wall!"

Secret took a second to register Victoria's comments. It clicked! *This bitch has been fucking in my damn house?* She lunged over Motherdear.

"We are all here for Tarron's sake," Mother-dear interjected, separating them. "He's not going to get better if you two start fighting in this hospital. Hell, they might even put him out because of the other patients' safety."

Victoria turned to see two burly security guards walking down the hallway behind her. Only the thoughts of Tarron lying in that hospital bed were playing full screen in her head.

Everyone was at a standstill when the emergency light at the nurses' station went off. The nurses rushed past Victoria and shouted for Secret and her friends to move.

They scurried into the room and closed the door. For the first time Victoria and Secret were standing only inches away from one another but they were not arguing or fighting. The worry about Tarron's health took precedence over their hatred for one another.

The wait was excruciating for all those who were staring at the solid wood door. The nurses were in the room for only a few short minutes. Tarron had accidentally pulled one of the cords out of the socket, which caused the alarm.

Still, to those waiting in that hallway, it seemed as if time was standing still. The nurse's explanation of what went on gave little ease to their sunken hearts.

Victoria knew at that point, Motherdear

was right. This was not the place or time for dealing with Secret. The only thing that mattered was Tarron's health. So she decided to leave. She hugged Motherdear and told her she'd wait for Tarron at home.

Secret went back inside the room to check on Tarron. Motherdear told Victoria that she would call her later. Then she, too, went to be by her son's side.

Unfortunately, Victoria left feeling defeated. As she approached her car, her mouth dropped at the sight before her. All four tires on her Honda Accord had been split!

I'll fix that bitch, she thought.

Two weeks later Tarron was released from the hospital. Motherdear drove him home and walked him to his door, where Victoria was waiting with open arms. Tarron was still very sore, and it was apparent when Victoria hugged him firmly.

"I see you are in good hands. I'll come back tomorrow to check up on you," said Motherdear.

"Okay, Mom. I'll see you later." Motherdear was thrown off guard by Victoria's use of the word *mom.* Her face told it all; it scrunched up like a sponge.

Victoria used herself as a crutch and led

him into the condo. Several candles were burning, the best of Luther Vandross played softly in the background, and a five-course meal was on the glass dining table.

Tarron wasn't hungry, but he ate as much as he could so as not to offend Victoria. After only being able to take showers in the hospital, he wanted to soak in a hot tub. Victoria ran his bathwater and poured in some bath oil to bring a smile to Tarron's face.

She began to undress him. First, she carefully pulled his T-shirt over his head. She wrapped plastic around his arm cast, to protect it from the water. She helped him to the bed and began to remove his shoes. The sweatpants and underwear were next to come off. Victoria did the same wrap job on his leg cast.

It had been twelve days since she'd seen him. His body looked weak as she helped him into the crackling bubbles and warm Epsom salts. With his arm and leg hanging over the tub, Tarron leaned back, but the back of the tub was cold. Victoria used her hands to push some warm water against the tub to warm it for him.

Tarron again leaned back and tried to find a comfortable position. When Victoria saw he was ready, she turned on the whirlpool jets to massage his weakened body.

Victoria left the bathroom to get Tarron a glass of water so he could take his medicine. The phone rang, it was Motherdear, and she wanted to make sure Tarron had taken his medicine. It made Victoria laugh when she hung up the phone.

"Baby, you are so lucky to have a mother like Motherdear," Victoria said.

Tarron didn't respond.

"Baby, did you hear me?"

Still there was no answer.

Victoria began to walk faster to the bathroom. When she opened the door, she found Tarron asleep. She had to wake him. It was time for his pills. She paused to watch him. The water swirled around, and the bubbles were piling up on his sides.

Victoria used a sponge to drop water onto his exposed chest. She smiled.

"Honey, you have to wake up. It's time for your medicine."

Tarron opened his eyes to find Victoria staring at him with those beautiful eyes and sexy lips. He opened his mouth, and she fed him his pills. She handed him the water and turned to leave.

"Hey, sweetie, come here. I have something to tell you." Victoria came back and kneeled down next to the tub. "It hurts to talk. You have to come closer to my mouth, so I can whisper."

Victoria bent over. She placed her ear inches away from his mouth. Tarron slowly pulled her into the tub—shoes, clothes, and all. Victoria was more concerned than upset. She didn't want to hurt him or have him hurt himself.

"Girl, I've missed you something terrible. I'm sorry about the drama you had to go through with Secret at the hospital. But the divorce will be final soon."

Victoria blushed. "It's not your fault. She's hurt. Your mother made me realize that."

"You know we'll have to get the children on the weekends." Tarron watched Victoria's reaction. "I have to spend more time with my son."

"Our son," Victoria responded. The water felt good. Being back in Tarron's arms felt even better. She decided to remove her soaked clothing and cuddle up next to her man.

Chapter 19

The football team was having its end-of-the-year cookout. Although it had been only a week since Tarron's casts were removed, he was excited about returning to his son's activities. As he pulled up to the park, he noticed Terrance swinging on the monkey bars with a few of his teammates. The older players from the one-hundred-pound team enjoyed a water balloon fight.

As Tarron headed in the direction of the jungle gym, one of the balloons sailed past its mark and splattered on the bar where Terrance hung like a monkey. Tarron watched as his son tried to get a tighter grip on the pole. He took off running but knew he was too many feet away. Tarron's heart sank as he gazed at Terrance's hand slipping away, one finger at a time. He came crashing down on his head. A large gash formed on his forehead. Blood spouted onto the foam carpet of the playground. At first, screams from the other children alerted the parents sitting off in the shade areas. And then came a hush over the entire park.

Tarron was running at top speed to his son's side. Luckily, an ambulance was already on the park grounds. They rushed to his side and gave him immediate care. Seconds later, they rushed Terrance off to Children's Hospital.

Terrance lost a lot of blood. The doctor came out and told Secret and Tarron that he would need a blood transfusion to have a chance at making it. The only problem was that he had a rare type of blood. The hospital did not have it in stock. They had been calling all the hospitals and blood banks in the area ... but no luck. The good thing was that both parents were there and one should be the same blood type. Both of them would have to be tested to see who could be a donor.

The doctor took Secret and Tarron to the nurses' station to have their blood drawn and tested. The nurse led them to the back to wait for the results. Fifteen minutes later, the door opened and the doctor came in, carrying a cream folder.

"We have a problem, Mr. and Mrs. Jenkins."

Tarron stood up. "What problem?"

"How can I say this? There is no easy way of putting it, so I'll give it to you direct."

"Doctor, what is it?" Secret shouted. Secret thought that maybe she had lost her little boy. She began to cry hysterically.

"Tarron, your blood type is A. Your wife's blood is type A. But your son is AB negative."

"What does that mean? I'm so confused," shouted Secret.

"It means that you can't be the boy's father." He pointed to Tarron.

"What?" Tarron punched the waiting room wall.

"I'm sorry you had to find out like this, but we need to find the real father now. Mrs. Jenkins, do you have any idea who the father of your son is?"

"It's Tarron's brother, Jay." Secret clenched her teeth, as if to brace herself for Tarron's explosion.

Tarron went ballistic. He began to knock over chairs and kick tables. Suddenly, he reached for his cell phone and called Jay. No answer.

"Secret, give me your cell phone!" Tarron snatched the phone from her hand and dialed Jay's number again.

Jay picked up. "Hey, sexy," he answered.

"Jay, don't hang up. It's Tarron. There's been an accident involving Terrance. Terrance is in real trouble. You have to get over here to Children's emergency room right away."

"I'm on my way." Jay slipped on his jeans and rushed out the door.

Tarron threw Secret's cell phone in the chair beside her. The thump made Secret remove her hands from over her face and look up into Tarron's crying eyes.

"I can't believe this shit!"

Secret, too afraid to speak, just lowered her head.

Shortly after, Jay rushed through the automatic doors of the emergency room. A nurse hurried him to the nurses' station to take his blood. Tarron stood in the corner with his hands pressed against the wall. Jay walked up to him after the nurse finished.

"Tarron, what is going on?"

Tarron looked at Jay with so much anger in his eyes. It took everything inside him not to punch Jay in his face. Instead, he said nothing. He only shook his head back and forth and then laid his head against his forearms on the wall. This topped the charts. He was prepared to disown his brother for life.

The doctor walked up. His facial expression was different from the first time he entered the waiting room.

246

"We have a match," said the doctor. "We need to get you into surgery right away, Mr. Jenkins." He pointed at Jay.

Tarron turned but realized that he was pointing at his brother. As Jay followed the doctor, Tarron kicked the end table display cabinet that held some information pamphlets. Jay gave one last look back, but his eyes didn't see Tarron. They found Secret curled up in a chair, still sobbing.

Minutes turned to hours. Tarron gazed into the presurgery room and saw Jay and Terrance lying side by side. It tore him up inside. It concerned him more that he could not save Terrance, rather than the fact that he was not his son.

Motherdear had arrived. "Excuse me. I'm looking for my son, Mr. Jenkins."

"Uh, right this way, ma'am." The nurse hesitated. She gave Motherdear a strange glare before escorting her to Terrance's room.

"Lord, why that look, honey? Oh, I pray everything's all right," Motherdear said, stroking her head.

Motherdear paused for a minute. Then the lightbulbs flashed in her mind like the Fourth of July. *The truth is finally out,* she thought.

"Tarron Jenkins is in the waiting room. Jay Jenkins is in the surgery room with Terrance

Jenkins, who's getting a blood transfusion," the nurse said.

Motherdear followed the signs on the wall to the waiting room. When she entered the door, she saw Tarron crying in a chair on one side and Secret doing the same in another.

"Oh, Lord . . ." Motherdear shook her head. "The shit done hit the fan." She ran to Secret first. Motherdear held her in her arms and squeezed until more water fell from Secret's eyes. She sat down in the chair next to Tarron and began rubbing his back.

Tarron's face tightened; his hands clenched. He watched the doctor as he walked toward them.

"Is my son going to be all right?" asked Secret.

"The next forty-eight hours are the critical ones," the doctor responded. "He will have to stay in the ICU for that period, and then we will move him to his own room, if everything goes well."

"Can I see him?" Secret asked.

"He's sleeping right now. But I guess you can peek in on him for a brief minute." The doctor flipped Terrance's medical chart and headed down the hall.

The nurse escorted Secret to the ICU room 3A. It broke her heart to see her little man hooked up to all those machines. The oxygen tubes in his nose upset her the most. She stood by his bedside and began to stroke his hair.

"Baby, your momma messed up real bad, and I don't know if I can do anything to fix it, either."

She leaned down to kiss his head. Teardrops fell onto his cheek. He looked so peaceful. She thought back to the day she gave birth.

Secret and Tarron were in the basement of a house they were renting in the upper northwest area of D.C. There was a major ice storm that covered the entire D.C., Maryland, and Virginia area.

They were watching *Do the Right Thing* when Secret felt a sharp pain. She blamed it on the Chinese food from earlier. The best part of the movie was getting good when the pain hit again.

As she stood to go to the bathroom, she realized her water broke. Tarron flipped out. He ran to get Secret's bag, realizing he forgot to help her up the stairs.

Tarron ran outside to start the car but slipped on the icy porch and bounced down four huge steps. Secret wanted to laugh but focused on her Lamaze breathing techniques.

Eventually, Tarron successfully led Secret to the car.

Doing about five miles an hour, they drove to Washington Hospital Center. Tarron left Secret in the car as he ran screaming, "I'm having a baby. I'm having a baby."

The nurses wheeled Secret inside, and Tarron spent the next three hours pacing as the doctors waited for Secret to dilate to ten centimeters. Tarron had to feed ice chips to Secret as he massaged her back. Then they had to walk the halls so the baby would drop.

The pain was incredible, but Secret would have nothing to do with an epidural, even though Tarron suggested it. Secret was in labor for eighteen hours before she gave birth to a seven-pound nine-ounce boy, whom Tarron immediately bonded with. Terrance, he called him.

Now, eight years later, she was back in the hospital praying to God to save her child. Eighteen hours to give birth, but only mere seconds for her to almost lose him.

The nurse broke her train of thought when she told Secret time was up. Secret bent over and kissed her son again. On her way back to the waiting room, she came across Jay lying in a bed in the recovery room. She stood at the door and stared at Jay. She thought, *Thank you! Thank you so much!*

When Secret got back to the waiting room, the doctor was advising Tarron to go home and get some sleep. Tarron wasn't about to leave *his* son. *He needs his father more than ever before,* he thought.

Chapter 20

Tarron needed to take a walk. He really just wanted to get away from Secret in the tight-sized waiting room. He went out front to get some fresh air. As he leaned up against the side of the building, his mind began to wonder. *Why me? I was the best at everything I did in life—everything except choosing the right wife.*

Jay had come around, and his nicotine habit got the best of him. He felt slightly dizzy when he stood at first. Jay collected himself and took five slow steps toward the door. Before grabbing his jacket, he yanked the Band-Aid from his arm, snatching his hair along with it. "Shit," he yelled. Jay tossed it to the ground and felt around his jacket pocket for his lighter. To his surprise . . . no lighter. *Someone outside will have one,* he thought.

Outside, he approached the shadow of a man standing in the corner of the hospital entrance. "Yo, man, can I get a light?"

Tarron stepped out from the shadows. "I don't smoke."

Jay's eyes widened when Tarron spoke.

"How could you?" The words surged from Tarron's lips.

"It was a long time ago, Tee."

"I can care less about you fucking Secret. I mean, how could you not tell me?"

"You were so happy when you wrote me in prison. Then, when I saw you with my own eyes, I didn't want to hurt you by telling you the girl I'd smashed off was the same girl you were married to. I know I'm foul, but I figured that telling you when I got home from prison was cruel. Come on, switch places."

"You've always wanted to be me. Things always worked out in my favor. Admit it, you were always envious that God gave me the better life."

"Hold up. I never wanted to be you. You forgot . . . I got tons of bitches. I was doing shit you never even dreamed of doing. I never cared about school. Fuck grades. I only went because the bitches were there. And Momma gave me more attention because I was always in trouble. You got the game all twisted."

"Then why did you send me all those e-mails telling me little clues to shit that involved you and Secret? Why didn't you just man up and tell me face-to-face?"

"I know you got the game fucked up. Me, send you an e-mail? What could I send it on? My ass . . . You know I don't have a computer. You think I'm gonna search the world, looking for a computer to e-mail you shit that I don't even know myself?"

"You didn't know that Secret wasn't going to ever tell me about you and her? You didn't know that the blood would tell me that the boy I raised from birth was not my son, but your son?"

"We made a pact not to tell you about us at that cookout, but hell no, did I ever think that Terrance was my son. I'm shocked about all of this, just like you," Jay lied.

"Yeah, right!"

"Fuck you, then, nigga. It happened, okay? Now stop acting like a little girl. See, I'm used to dealing with bullshit. I can . . . We can handle this, and the right way. Stop crying and think about a solution."

"Fuck you. . . ."

"Fuck me. . . . Naw, fuck you," Jay yelled.

"Momma was right. She said if you ever found out, then you wouldn't see it as us trying to protect you. You would turn this into a *Tarron* saga. Just for the record . . . it's not all about you."

"Momma knew about you and Secret?" Tarron's face frowned.

"I had to talk to someone when I realized who Secret was at the cookout."

"I don't know anybody no more. Is this a conspiracy to fuck up Tarron because he has it all and done it all?"

Tarron bumped Jay as he walked back through the hospital doors.

On his drive home, the devastation of the previous event had Tarron's mind in a whirlwind. It took him longer than usual to reach home, because he drove twenty miles per hour, stuck in a daze. Tarron reached his door but sat in the car for minutes before exiting. When he finally collected himself, he stumbled out of the car as if he'd been drinking with the boys. Tarron pushed his key in the hole and slammed the door behind him. Going to bed was his only comfort. He never even removed his clothes. Tarron slid beneath the covers and fell into a deep sleep. The images played inside his head just like in the movie *The Best Man*. Nightmares plagued his brain. The entire scene of the night Secret and Jay met replayed in detail in Tarron's mind.

There is Secret, sitting in the booth with her girlfriends, heads rolling back and forth, laughing at the acts being carried out by one another. Jay glides across the path of Secret and her girlfriends in the nightclub. Slowly, a hand rises into the air and a finger points Jay out to Secret. Secret stands to her feet. She turns in her crocheted little tennis skirt. Her long, thick legs begin to step one after the other. Each step has confidence, banging against the marble tile.

Her right hand taps Jay's right shoulder. She leans in close to him. He tastes her sweet lips. Secret begins to whisper in his ear. An enormous smile takes over Jay's face. She leads him out through the maze of crowded people, with no one suspecting that very soon these two strangers will be locked in lust.

They turn left after leaving the club, then another whisper into Jay's ear, and they make a quick U-turn. Their bodies are even closer. Jay's arm is wrapped around her waist; his hand in her ass. Tarron's images were so detailed, he could see the wind blowing Secret's skirt, the strings hanging off her blouse, and even the style of her hair.

They step into a deep doorway, blind to everyone except Tarron. He watches as Jay slides his hand up the back of her thigh and grabs a handful of Secret's ass. Secret's eyes close as he sucks down on her neck, teasing her with his nervous tongue.

Secret pulls out a condom from between her breasts and places it in Jay's hand. He rips the condom from the wrapper and frantically tries to open his jeans. Slowly, he pinches the rubber and rolls it over his shaft.

Secret shifts her thong to the side, being very careful not to destroy it. Jay moves in again. Secret blocks him with her right forearm. She turns around and places both hands on the gray and white concrete. Her back arches and her firm ass is exposed.

Jay pushes up her skirt, moves his hard penis up and down her clitoris to separate her lips. Firmly, he enters her. Secret, already very moist, receives him readily. Jay locks on to her hips. He moves faster and faster. Her ass is beginning to make that clapping sound.

Jay bends his knees so that his penis smacks her walls from different angles. The wind carries her slight moans.

Secret told Tarron that it lasted only a few minutes. But in Tarron's imagination, it lasted much longer. He watched as her hair flew. He watched as her ass jiggled. He watched as her facial expression changed with each thrust. The thoughts sickened him as well as excited him. The blood rushed to his pelvic muscles. His pulse rate increased, and he started to sweat. The pumping caused not only Tarron to move, but Victoria as well.

Tarron's tossing and turning awakened Victoria. She rolled over to see the sweaty face of Tarron and the pup tent he had going on below. Victoria believed that she could never let a hard dick go to waste, so she pulled back the covers.

She circled the head of his hard pole with her tongue. Imitating his brother's movement, he moved his body up and down. As Jay's pole went into Secret, his shaft went into Victoria.

Victoria used more force, sucking his shaft deeper into her mouth. Her nails locked into Tarron's thighs. She adjusted her body to get a more comfortable position to take his entire shaft. When she slid his penis out and slurped up his left testicle, Tarron awoke to the sensational chill that went up his body.

His eyes opened to find Victoria's ass bent next to him and his left ball engulfed in her mouth. The vibration from her humming caused chills to form. He pulled on the sheets, because he was reaching climax. Victoria knew he was close. She immediately went back to his throbbing penis.

His juices were ready to burst. She sucked

from the bottom all the way to the slit at the head. The feeling was incredible. He exploded in her mouth. Nearly choking, she still kept going. She couldn't stop.

His penis went limp, and she kept going. The beast came out of Victoria. She knew exactly how to make his penis hard again. She kept going. Victoria would not stop. Tarron tried to pull his penis out of her, but again she would not stop, sucking with more and more force.

Tarron pulled her hair. She would not stop. Tarron exploded again, but this time with greater force. Victoria was doing a downward motion when his cum shot into her mouth. She had to stop.

It surprised her. It was a large amount. This time, she fully choked. It was too much to swallow. She spit every ounce onto the patch of Tarron's pubic hair. Tarron was exhausted. By the time she was able to catch her breath and was ready for more, Tarron was snoring loudly. She punched him and went on to satisfy herself.

Nearly three weeks had gone by. Terrance was sent home and was back to being his old self. Tarron was not. He dove headfirst into his work, taking on very time-consuming new deals.

Victoria tried to be a supportive girlfriend but was confused about how to deal with his change in behavior. Tarron had canceled his two weekends with the children—arguing that he had too much work to do.

Victoria was beginning to feel the stress of Tarron's absence. She rolled around night after night in an empty bed. Whenever she touched a new area, the chill of the sheets woke her. It then took several minutes, sometimes hours, for her to fall back asleep.

There were many nights when she lay in bed counting the cracks on the ceiling wishing Tarron would walk through the bedroom door. Her wishes went ungranted. She felt like she was losing him. *This is definitely too much for one man to handle.* In her heart, Victoria knew Tarron's ultimate desire was to have a son. She remembered him saying that when Terrance was born, that was the best day of his life. While Tarron loved Tika very much, if Terrance were his only child, he'd be fine with that. Victoria felt somewhat responsible. *What can I do? Is there any repair for a man who found out that the son he loved so much was really not his son, but in fact his nephew?*

Victoria knew the anger that burned inside

him. After all, his family had gone from picture-perfect to a season finale of *Jerry Springer: Secrets Mates Never Tell.* Victoria realized Tarron hid his feelings over the whole deal inside his work. *I guess men aren't supposed to cry,* she thought.

Tarron's emotions were numb, so numb he could not feel Victoria's anger when he spoke to her on the phone. No longer was she talking to him; now she was screaming at him.

"Look, I'm trying to understand your situation, but I need to be taken care of, too!" Victoria's eyes quickly filled with teardrops from the pain.

Tarron could understand her point of view. He knew her plea wasn't that much. "Victoria, baby, I'm sorry. I'm dealing with a lot. I promise to make up to you later."

Victoria slammed down the phone.

It had been three months since the hospital drama. Jay had skipped the last two poker nights with the boys. Tarron ignored all of Jay's attempted pages. Tarron was sinking, and deep.

His special getaway with Victoria was steadily approaching. Tarron was looking forward to his trip to the Caribbean. It was what he needed. He had been neglecting the woman he loved and had planned to give Victoria the ring he'd purchased along with Secret's anniversary gift. Victoria put all the travel plans in order.

A quick limousine ride to the dock and aboard the Royal Caribbean ship they hopped. Attentive to all the ship's features, Victoria oohed and aahed. Tarron, on the other hand, wasn't paying much attention to Victoria's detailed description of the boat. He found himself lost. Tarron wanted to be seduced by the movements of her lips. His desire to become the old Tarron again was strong. Standing on the edge of the deck, he rubbed Victoria's right thigh.

All he wanted to do was make love to her. Even at the set sails party on the top deck, Tarron seemed unimpressed with the departure celebration. He could only focus his energy on Victoria.

Tarron rested his hand on her butt and gently kissed her on the neck. This startled her a little, because she was so deep into throwing streamers over the rail and waving good-bye to complete strangers on the dock.

"Sweetie, let's go to our suite," he whispered in her ear.

As she turned to face him, she saw a look in his eyes that she couldn't recall ever seeing before. The look told her the entire story. She knew exactly every erotic detail that raced through his mind. Tarron looked intently at her because he still couldn't believe she was real.

She wanted to feel all the desire his body language gave off. The want in his eyes made her wonder, *Right here, right now?*

She kissed him forcefully. The loud ship's horn sounded off as fireworks exploded in the clear sky. That kiss was different for both of them. So much passion was released, it caused Victoria's body to shake. Victoria's loins began to pulsate.

Her clitoris shared the tease Tarron's wet tongue played with her lips. Their lips pressed harder, and she tightened her swollen inner walls to cause pressure on her clit. By the second blast of the loud horn, she was reaching her climax. She needed . . . she wanted more.

Victoria dragged them through crowds of people who were enjoying the fireworks. She rushed him back to their suite. Usually the foreplay was symbolic of passionate lovemaking, but not that day. They were more like animals.

She ripped his cream short-sleeved shirt, popping all the buttons with one motion. Again, she pressed her lips forcefully against him, backing him against the suite door. The

264

bang of his head hitting the door sent Tarron into a rage.

He yanked her hair in revenge. He spun her around and pushed her into the cherry oak dresser. Pressing her face onto the dresser, he lifted her little miniskirt and tore off her G-string. The wrestle with his belt on his linen slacks took only a minute. He pulled out his hard penis, and without even waiting for his slacks and underwear to fall to his ankles, Tarron thrust his erect shaft into her moist garden from the doggy-style position.

Victoria let out a short scream as his dick penetrated her pussy's inner core. Yanking back her hair gave him all the leverage he needed to pound that pussy harder and harder. Victoria tried to push up from the dresser, but Tarron only pushed her body back into position.

Victoria pushed with all her might and caused Tarron's dick to pop out and sent him back against the suite door. She took the offensive again. She jumped into his arms and wrapped her legs around his back. Tarron maneuvered his dick back inside her. Tarron started to lift her up and down on top of his dick. He began to flex his muscles by walking around the suite, still moving his dick in and out.

Before she could complain about her hands slipping from around his neck and her fear of falling back, Tarron began to trip over his pants and underwear, which were tangled around his feet. He lifted Victoria up off his dick and threw her onto the bed. Tarron was bending over to pull his legs out of his clothing when he went flying toward the bed.

Victoria had snuck behind him and pushed him. Tarron went stumbling and fell just before hitting the bed. Lying on the floor, still tangled in his pants, he rolled over. Victoria was already in position to straddle him. She jammed his dick back inside her.

Victoria grabbed his head and pressed her 34C breasts in his face. Holding the back of his head gave her the leverage to ride his horse like a Western cowgirl breaking in a stallion from the wild. Her thighs were dripping with her womanly juices, and the more she squeezed and bounced on his shaft, the juicier it became.

She pulled back in a quick motion, causing his stallion to fall out again. Grabbing the center of his underwear and pants, she dragged him across the floor until he had enough room to lie fully back. She dashed up and sat her thick waterfall on his unsuspecting mouth. Victoria loved fucking his face. Grinding her hips as he tried to lick, suck, and bite made it hard at times for him to breathe.

Finally, Tarron reached for her hair and pulled with all his might. Victoria lost her balance and hit her head on the little table. Fighting for air, he became enraged.

He leaped on top of her without giving a time-out for her injury. He pulled her legs up over her head, making her toes touch the floor above her head. Then he smashed his stallion back into her stable. He began to fuck her with all his might, until she was trying to bite and begging for him to stop. He would stop for a second, then pound a little more. Tears began to form beneath her eyelids from the pain, which was becoming unbearable.

Tarron switched positions.

Victoria once again jammed his dick into her pussy and started riding his limp penis. Her facial expression said everything. *What the hell is this?* "I don't know where the old Mr. Jenkins went, but I want him back," Victoria said, eyes glued to Tarron.

Chapter 21

Terrance had been out of the hospital for over three months, and Tarron continued to struggle with the news that he had fathered only one child. In spite of his vacation with Victoria, the tension was thick between them. So thick, Tarron not giving her the ring was never a second thought.

The alarm blasted loudly through the speakers, unnerving him. He rolled out of bed, not even acknowledging Victoria's presence with a glance. Tarron spent an extra twenty minutes standing under the hot, body-piercing shower. The drive to work was done in complete silence, except for the sounds of the outside world.

Shanice knew what the dark pair of sunshades meant. It was the price he paid for either a long night out with the boys or . . . He went straight into his office, with only a slight wave to Shanice. He was sitting with his face buried in his hands when his elbow tapped the mouse.

YOU'VE GOT MAIL.

Tarron looked up to find that he had several e-mails waiting for him. He scrolled down to a familiar name.

Click.

Tarron, it hurts me to know that you are in love with someone else. When I see couples holding hands or families spending time together, it makes me want to cry.

I find myself dreaming about our past life, when we used to do simple things like watch planes take off and land. That seems like so many years ago.

I know we all have skeletons in our closets, but who would have known that an entire cemetery would have been dug up?

My past is something that no matter how hard I wish I could go back and change, I know I can't. You, of all people, should be able to relate to wanting to go back and change things in your past. But neither of us can. But putting me on death row because of a situation that happened before we even met is just wrong.

I love you with all of my heart, and I still believe that we should be together. It is the conflict between us that has made you find solitude with your so-called soul mate. But if you were to search your heart, it should be my face in which you find comfort. I had to search my heart once before, when you went outside our marriage, and you asked me for forgiveness. Now it's my turn to ask you for that same chance to correct a terrible mistake.

I love you and need you just as much as I need air. Losing you and your love is suffocating me. Find the compassion to save my life.

Give me back my air so I can breathe again.

Secret

Tarron felt guilty for all his extramarital activities with other women. One that could have sent Secret over the edge was the time he slept with one of her friends. Tarron tried to fight back the memory but couldn't. As he leaned back in his chair, all the nasty details unfolded. He knew exactly which incident Secret referred to.

It was the summer prior to their three-year anniversary. Tarron and the guys had ridden their motorcycles into Myrtle Beach for Bike Week. Kurt, Ray, Tweet, and Tarron were checking into their hotel rooms when he noticed Secret's friend Pinkey and three of her girlfriends getting off the hotel elevator.

His first thought was that his weekend was shot. He knew that Secret would quickly find out about his activities on this trip.

Later that same night, when they were leaving a party at one of the local nightclubs, he felt someone hop on the back of his motorcycle at a streetlight. When he turned to see who it was, Pinkey was getting comfortable and reaching for his extra helmet. He was shocked.

"Me and my girls want a ride."

Tarron looked around to see all her friends in position. The light turned green and off his boys pulled. Tarron lowered his visor and hit the gas.

Yelling for him to go faster, Pinkey squeezed Tarron tighter. Tarron clicked into third gear and pulled the front wheel up into the air, causing her to bury her face in his back and hold on for dear life.

Tarron felt her soft, soft nipples harden as her breasts pressed against his back. They ended up at a little bar on the beach across from their hotel rooms. All eight of them played drinking games until the bar closed for the night.

Even though the lights flicked, the girls weren't ready to call it a night. They still wanted to party. Kurt suggested that everyone go upstairs to his room, where he had more drinks. Tarron wasn't worried about having them come up to the hotel room, because this was Secret's friend and he wasn't going to do anything wrong around Pinkey.

Four drinks later, they all decided on a sexual arousal.

Tweet made one girl take off all her clothes and walk to the elevator at the end of the hallway and press the down button, then walk back to the room. She didn't hesitate for a minute, and she went straight to the grind. "No problem," she said, stripping down to nothing.

One girl convinced Kurt to lick her friend, starting at her left ankle, up her leg, around her vagina, down her right leg, and stopping at her right ankle. The drinks were in full effect, because he did it and even gave her a few soft puffs of air into her vagina before moving on down the other leg.

Tweet and the young lady with the birth-mark on her face hit the closet, and she allowed him to do whatever he wanted to do to her for two minutes. They went in, and Ray counted down the time from outside the door. When there were about thirty seconds left, he snatched open the door and exposed Tweet, down on his knees with her right breast in his mouth and his left hand in her panties.

"Hell yeah! That's the shit I'm talking about," Ray shouted.

"Michelle, let me find out you ain't nothing but a freak when you're out of town," screamed Pinkey.

"What happens at Bike Week stays at Bike Week," she replied, laughing. Tweet's hand was still fondling her wetness.

The game kept going, and it was really starting to heat up. Tarron was tired of playing the nice guy, so when it was his turn, he made Ray go into the bedroom and lie down on the bed with his eyes closed. The rule was to let any two of the girls do whatever they wanted to do.

"It's like that, dog?" said Ray. "You just wait."

Ray stood up and pulled his pants up, then ran and jumped on the bed. Brittany and Dee-Dee walked in after him and closed the door. At first the others could hear laughter, but that turned into melodies of groans. Pinkey ran over to peek through the keyhole, but all she could see was the bed moving back and forth, up and down.

She tried to open the door, but they had locked it from inside. Two minutes turned into four, then eight, and finally after Tweet started banging on the door, Brittany opened it. All three laughed.

"You were in there for almost twenty minutes. What they do to you?" asked Tweet.

"What happens here stays here? I won't tell—at least not until they're gone," Ray said.

Kurt then decided that he had had enough with the playing around. He was ready to get buck naked and fuck. "I want every girl to put her name on a piece of paper and put it into this glass, and every nigga to put his name on a piece of paper and their name into this other glass, and whoever's name you pull, that's the person you go off with to your own private space," he yelled.

Michelle pulled Tweet's name. Kurt selected Dee-Dee. Ray pulled Brittany. Tarron and Pinkey just looked at each other, because they knew that their names were the only ones left. The others quickly grabbed a bottle, then rolled out with their partner.

Tarron looked at Pinkey again and laughed.

He reached into the glasses and pulled out the two pieces of paper. He balled the sheets into small fake basketballs and tried to shoot them in the wastebasket near the bathroom door. After missing both shots, he walked over and slam-dunked them into the can as he went to make a deposit to the porcelain bank.

When Tarron walked out of the bathroom, he found himself in a dimly lit room. Pinkey was lying on her stomach, facing the foot of the bed, watching television. Tarron paused for a second and examined her beautiful body shining from the glow of the soft lights.

Starting with her feet, his eyes walked their way upward toward her thick, but firm thighs. Next was the juicy, plump butt. Pinkey turned to catch Tarron checking her out. He realized he was busted.

"I hope you don't mind that I made myself comfortable."

"Naw, I don't mind. Would you like another drink before I get comfortable?"

"Sure, why not?"

Tarron fixed a drink for her and another for himself. He kept thinking about how sexy she looked stretched out across the sheets. He knew he shouldn't drink anymore, but his manly urges got the best of him.

"Here you go, Pinkey."

"Tarron, you can change the channel if you

want. This is a repeat, and I've seen it several times."

"That's all right. I like this show."

"Me too. Raymond is so funny," Pinkey said, playfully moving her feet over the comforter.

Tarron sat on his bed with his back against the headboard. They both continued to drink until the bottle was empty. Tarron muted the television, because he heard a strange noise. There were moans coming from next door, where Ray had taken Brittany. The moans came in a variety of pitches—slow, steady moans; then short, rapid moans. Each was followed by a constant banging against the wall.

Pinkey turned to look at Tarron, and they both started laughing. Tarron turned to lean back against the wall, causing a sudden pain in his back.

"Ow!" shouted Tarron as he reached for his back.

"What's wrong?"

"This pain. I think I caught a cramp in my back."

"Would you like for me to massage it?"

Tarron didn't respond right away. Even though he knew better, the pain was now shooting across his back at a higher level. He slowly rolled over onto his stomach and agreed to the massage.

Pinkey played it cool by first rubbing his

back through his shirt. "I need to get to your skin. Is that okay?" she asked.

Tarron nodded. She slid his shirt up to just below his head. Her hands were cold with the first touch to his bare skin, but they quickly warmed up as she moved up and down his back.

"Tarron, do you have any massage oil?"

"I have some baby oil on the dresser, in my black shower bag."

She poured a large amount into the palm of her hand. Pinkey then massaged the oil into his back using a circular motion. Her hands were so soft. Pinkey could feel how tense he was as she manipulated the tender spots of his back.

Tarron closed his eyes, and the many drinks made the room start to spin around in his head. Not only was the massage feeling good, but the liquor was kicking in. The two of them together caused Tarron to doze off.

Twenty minutes into his rest, Tarron felt his shorts come off. He opened his eyes, and Pinkey posed naked over him. She watched him for a second before going straight to work. She quickly wrapped her mouth around his erect penis and began sucking with the pressure of a Hoover upright.

Tarron grabbed her long black hair with every intention of pulling his shaft out of her mouth, but those manly urges, those damn manly urges, got the best of him, and instead of pulling his penis out of her mouth, he only assisted her by bobbing her head up and down.

Tarron climaxed. She wasn't done. Friend or not, Pinkey was going all the way. She gave Tarron a minute to regroup. Eager to show off her talent, she tore off the wrapping of a condom and placed it on his penis as she placed his testicles inside her mouth. The vibration of her lips kept his penis as hard as a rock as she unrolled the condom all the way down his shaft.

Tarron and Pinkey made eye contact as she climbed up to straddle him. She began with a slow reggae dance motion. Pinkey took control in a perfect position to dominate his penis, as if she was the man in the encounter. Faster and faster she went.

Tarron grabbed the sheets as his headboard was now pounding the wall. Pinkey moaned louder as she reached her first orgasm. He could feel the warm womanly juices hit the base of his shaft.

He slid his legs onto the floor, keeping her on top of him. Tarron reached under her thick thighs and, in one quick motion, lifted her into the air. He used her thighs to bounce her up and down his shaft. Pinkey's moans turned into screams of delight. Tarron hit every spot inside. Pinkey felt a second orgasm approaching. Tarron did not stop. He just kept pounding his hard shaft in and out of her until the third orgasm had come full circle.

Tarron turned her toward the bed and laid her down softly. He removed his securely wrapped penis from her pulsating vagina, but still she wanted more. *Damn, Secret's friend is a fiend,* he thought.

He hit it doggy style. She thought she was ready. He slipped his finger in her anus to prepare for *big daddy*. Pinkey enjoyed the feeling. But the pleasure quickly turned into a sharp pain.

"Relax, baby. It'll get better the more you're opened."

Pinkey smiled. She was no virgin to anal sex. After ten minutes of being worked from behind, she felt a new sensation. Her body quivered.

The intense shaking excited Tarron, too. He started smacking her cheeks hard. Tarron pushed deeper and deeper into her with every stroke. Pinkey's moans quickly escalated to screams. Tarron knew he was hitting it right when he began to hear the little fart sounds coming from the air trying to escape his long stroke. He went deep.

Pinkey yelled, "More!"

When she thought he was finished, he snatched her by her hair and unloaded an oversized amount of cum inside the condom. He was exhausted. He released her hair, and both of them fell, drained, to the bed.

YOU'VE GOT MAIL.

When Tarron returned from his daydream, his penis was as hard as nails. He moved his mouse to his new-e-mail button, which was blinking on his screen.

Click.

It's Me Again,

I hope you had a chance to read the first e-mail I sent. This one is just to ask you to give me a chance to speak with you face-to-face next week at the family reunion. Yes, I'm coming! Motherdear insisted.

He clicked out of the e-mail. Tarron never responded.

Chapter 22

Secret needed to treat herself to something good. Her recent circumstances had sucked the life right out of her. She decided to go shopping in Georgetown, which usually made her feel better. Despite her best attempts to look presentable, Secret's appearance revealed her grief. From her split ends to her loose-fitting Seven jeans, it was almost impossible for her to pull it together. The best make-up in her case couldn't hide her most noticeable flaws . . . the permanent bags beneath her eyes.

The children were off with Tarron at Six Flags in New Jersey, so this was a great time for her to focus on herself. Secret strolled past some of her favorite stores but saw nothing interesting. Pausing at a new Italian shoe store, she spotted a pair of multicolored leather-strapped sandals. Admiring several other pairs, she observed Victoria being fitted for the same multicolored shoes she adored. Secret walked through the door, and it chimed.

Victoria glanced up, and her eyes made contact with Secret. Victoria quickly rose to her feet, ignoring the salesman. No way was Secret going to sucker punch her a second time.

"I see we have the same taste in shoes as we do in men," Secret said.

Victoria did not respond. She only stood there with her fist clenched tightly, watching Secret's every move.

"I didn't come in here to fight or argue with you. Maybe we could talk. I want to get to know the woman who will be spending time with my children."

Victoria told the salesman to hold a pair of the shoes in a size eight and that she would get them when she returned. She grabbed her shopping bags and reluctantly followed Secret to the Starbucks across the street. They sat down at a small table near the picture-view window in front.

Secret sipped her Caffè Latte, and Victoria her Caramel Frappuccino. Both of them sat watching the movements of the other very carefully, for different reasons. Victoria wanted revenge for the hospital drama, and Secret needed answers to the many "why" questions running through her head. *Why her? Why Tarron? Why them?*

"So, Victoria, you are in the investment business," Secret stated, breaking the silence.

"I'm the assistant director of MetLife Investment Firm."

"That sounds very similar to Tarron's title."

"Our jobs are very similar. We just work for different companies. Much different from being a housewife, you know?" Victoria swallowed.

Secret ignored Victoria.

"I'm still not understanding why you invited me to have coffee with you."

"Vicki . . . Is it all right that I call you that?"

"Sure."

"Well, Vicki, I'm really not ready to call my marriage quits. But I have to face reality. When the entire truth comes out, there won't be anything on earth that will make Tarron stay with me, anyway."

"What's the entire story?"

"My story isn't why I asked you here. I want to know more about the woman who will probably be around my children on their weekends with their father. You know we're getting a divorce."

Victoria showed no emotion. "Secret, I love those children with all of my heart. I have to. You see, I'm not blessed to have children of my own. And Tarron's two blessings were brought to me by God to take the place of this empty hole in my life. I will never try to replace you as their mother or compete with you for their love, but I will love them more and more as we spend time together."

"It's funny, Vicki. I believe you will and do love my children, but the key words are *my children*. These children have a mother already—a damn good one. If by chance you and Tarron get any closer, you just remember that I'm their mother and will always be their mother." Secret appeared to be more hostile at this point. "Besides, I don't think Terrance wants to be around either of you."

The tone of the conversation immediately changed. Victoria sat taking a long sip of her drink. Her eyes stared right through Secret and watched her every move.

That last exchange and Victoria's long, silent stare signaled the need for a time-out. Secret decided to lighten the mood with a comment about those shoes.

"If you buy those shoes, then we can dress like twins one day," said Secret sarcastically.

"Now, why did you go and say something like that? I really wanted to buy those shoes, but there's no way in hell I'm buying them if you have them."

"That's a good thing, because I was getting them after we left," Secret said.

"I see you're trying to be a comedian."

Ray and a few of his bartenders were coming through the doors of Starbucks when he noticed Victoria and Secret. Ray hurried to find his cell phone and called Tarron.

"What up, fool?" Tarron said as he answered.

"Nigga, I hope you're sitting down."

"I'm driving on Fourth Street on my way home," said Tarron.

"You won't believe what I'm looking at right now."

"What?"

"Check this out. Victoria and Secret are down here at Starbucks on Wisconsin Avenue." Ray peeked to check the ladies once more.

"They're in the same store?"

"The same store. Shit, nigga, they're at the same table, talking 'bout yo black ass."

"You're bullshittin'." Tarron nearly drove himself off the road.

"I'm serious," Ray answered.

Tarron was at a loss for words. So many thoughts ran through his head. He almost crashed his car when he got a visual of both of them sipping coffee like old friends.

"Thanks, Ray. Good looking out. I'll holler at you later."

When Victoria returned home from shopping, Tarron was sitting on the edge of the couch. He startled her as she turned on the light in the living room.

"Where have you been?" he asked.

"You're asking like you already know."

"I do."

"Then what are you asking me for if you already know?"

"Baby, I need to know why you and my soon-to-be ex-wife are having coffee and acting like best friends."

"We were just clearing up a few things."

"What things?"

"She's giving you the divorce. She just wanted to know the woman her children will soon be around on a full-time basis."

"She's giving me the divorce?"

"With no strings attached," Victoria squealed. She leaped in his arms from joy.

Tarron had a funny feeling. He knew something wasn't right. He decided to tell Victoria about the e-mail with the unusual message that he received.

Chapter 23

It was the third Thursday of the month. Tweet, Ray, Kurt, and Jay were nestled around the card table. Tweet was dealing when suddenly Ray could no longer control himself.

"Jay, have you talked to your brother?"

"No, not since the night at the hospital."

"Man, how could you not tell him?"

Everyone was silent. They were waiting for his response. Their bodies froze in time.

"Well, it was a weird moment for me when I finally realized that Secret was the girl from the club. Remember, we even talked about it. We were at the bar, and I told you guys about this girl who banged me outside in a cut."

"Hell yeah, I remember," said Tweet.

"Then, while I was in jail, my brother came to visit. He was in there telling me about this girl that he was in love with and who passed the hooker trap."

"What's the hooker trap?" Kurt asked.

"The hooker trap is when one of the brothers starts falling for a girl. The brother sets up a chance meeting between that girl and a family member she has never met before in order to see if she would give him any play. If she gave out the number, then both of them would date her until they set up a meeting to see if she would fuck both of them. But Secret didn't give out her number. He knew she was the one." Jay walked over to the window and opened the curtain.

He continued. "I heard about the wedding from my mother when I called home. Tarron seemed to be so happy with Secret. They had dreams of a big family, the vacation getaways, the good-paying job, the big home, and they were living the American dream."

Jay scanned the room to watch the fellas' reactions. "Then I was released from jail. When Tarron introduced his family to me, I didn't even recognize Secret. It wasn't until later when we both realized we'd met. In more ways than one," he joked.

"That's foul!" shouted Tweet.

"By that time it seemed too late. Our moment together didn't justify ruining an entire foundation that was built on love. Many of the new twists and turns are all new to me as well. Who would have thought that my minutes of lust would have birthed a child that is being raised by my brother? Hell, I always wanted a son."

"Well, now you've got one," Ray said. "That's some deep white trailer-park trash shit."

"Now, what words would be proper to say when your nephew becomes your son, your niece is also your son's half sister, and your sister-in-law is your baby's momma?" Ray taunted.

The phone rang. It rang again.

"Tweet, answer the fucking phone," Ray shouted.

"Hello."

"Who is this?" Tarron asked.

"What you mean? You called my house. Who's this?" Tweet yelled.

"It's me."

"Me who?"

"Tarron, you bitch-ass nigga. Stop playing."

"You on your way?"

"Who there?" Tarron asked.

"Me, Kurt, Ray, and your brother. You coming over?"

"Hell no, me and that nigga share everything—the same mother, the same father, the same friends, the same blood, and even the same fucking baby mother. I'll be damn if we gonna share the same space! I'll holla back later," Tarron said as he slammed down the phone.

Then the line went dead. Tweet looked back at Jay and just shrugged his shoulders.

Ray kept pushing Jay for answers. "So, how was Secret?"

"I told you at the club. Shit, it was so long ago, and I was twisted. I really can't remember anything, but that it happened."

"Shit, if you can't remember if it was good or not, then it never happened," Kurt joked.

Jay looked at Kurt. "Tell that to my brother."

Chapter 24

Tarron was in the middle of a business call when his secretary buzzed his intercom to inform him that his wife, Secret, was on the line.

"Hello," Tarron answered impatiently.

"Tarron, I need you to talk to your son." Secret hesitated to let the words flow from her mouth.

"Well, when I have one, I will."

Secret's attitude changed at his response. "Oh, it's like that. Okay then, you need to talk to your nephew about school." She sucked her teeth.

"You know I really don't have time." Tarron paused. Despite everything that had happened, he loved Terrance. "Look, what's his problem with school?"

"One of the kids was clowning him about something that ticked him off, and he got into a fight."

"Did he win?" Tarron asked.

"That's not the point."

"All right, put him on the phone," Tarron said. He could sense her frustration with his comment.

"No. It needs to be a face-to-face talk."

Tarron was dealing with so many different emotions. On one hand, Terrance seemed to need him, and Secret referred to Terrance as his son. But still, the fact was, he wasn't. He was really his nephew.

There were visions of him and his brother standing together and Terrance running toward them screaming, "Daddy." They both hold out their arms, but he rushes into Jay's arms. Jay lifts him into the air and begins to spin him around until they both become dizzy and fall to the ground. Tarron just stands there, watching, as tears run down his face.

When Tarron pulled up at the house, he noticed the unkempt lawn. Terrance was sitting on the front porch, bouncing a ball against the wooden post. He looked up when he heard the car door close.

"I know you ain't coming to play, Daddy."

Terrance stood to his feet and looked deep into Tarron's eyes. He turned and ran inside the house.

Tarron didn't know what to expect, but he never pictured him running away from him or the disrespect.

Secret rushed to the door and saw Tarron coming down the walkway.

"You see what I mean?" shouted Secret.

Tarron walked past Secret without speaking or looking at her. She was disgusted but only walked in and closed the door. Tarron called for Terrance, but there was no reply. He slowly walked up the stairs and knocked on Terrance's bedroom door.

"Who is it?"

"It's me, boy. Don't play."

"Go away. We're not family anymore."

"Boy, I'm going to count to three, and if this door isn't open, I'm going to beat you like you owe me money. One, two . . ."

The door flew open, and Terrance stood with this little tough-boy look.

"You've been watching those made-for-TV white family movies again. Only thing is that shit doesn't work with little black kids. If you don't wipe that look off your face, the last thing you're going to see is me smacking the taste out of your mouth."

Terrance quickly erased the look. He walked over to his bed and sat down softly. He wasn't going to test any new boundaries. He could sense that things were very serious.

"You wanna explain what happened in school?"

"The fight wasn't my fault."

"What happened?" Tarron replied.

"We were at recess. I was killing Joe on the court. He got mad and started joning. I was frying him, and everyone was laughing. Then, then—"

"Then what?"

"Then he said that I was a bastard child. That my uncle was my daddy and my daddy was my uncle, and that my sister was my cousin, too."

"What?"

"He said that he heard his mother talking with my mother in their kitchen when Mommy was getting her hair done."

"Then what?"

"Everybody started laughing, and I stole him. He grabbed me and hit me. So I threw him on the ground and started kicking him. Then the teacher broke us up and took us to the office."

"My son, the Mike Tyson of the playground," he said, laughing.

"It ain't funny. I want you to be my daddy, not Uncle Jay. Why did you have to mess up our family?"

"Son, it's complicated. I won't even lie to you and tell you that I know what you're feeling, because I don't. The truth of the matter is that I'm just as messed up inside as you."

"You are?"

"Of course I am, but you don't see me fighting and acting as if I didn't have any home training."

"But . . ."

"But nothing. Terrance, you must understand that Jay is your biological father, and if I had known that from the very beginning, I still would've done most of the things I did for you."

"You would?"

"Yes. Since Jay was in prison, I would've been at all your birthday parties, picked you up to hang out, and whipped your butt when you got into trouble. I would've still been at every Little League game." Tarron looked Terrance in the eye. "I love you, and that will never change."

"But what do I call you?"

"I'm still your dad, so call me Dad." Tarron smiled.

He reached out, grabbed Terrance, and

pulled him close. He whispered that no matter what had happened, he'd always be around. Secret stood at the door and watched as they hugged. Although Terrance didn't resist, she could tell that he wasn't totally ready to forgive.

Chapter 25

A month had passed since Tarron and Terrance had had their little discussion. Tarron was very worried about Terrance. He wanted to spend more time with him but knew that might confuse the boy even more than he was already.

Tarron's background and his own personal relationship with his father made him question his decision. Having spent very little time with his father had caused major heartache for him growing up. He never wanted his own children to have to experience that part of his life. Tarron wanted a better relationship with his own children, but Terrance wasn't his child.

Tarron sat at the bar in the VIP lounge in the club. As he lowered his glass, he noticed Jay walking up behind him in the mirror of the bar.

"Brother, we need to talk," said Jay as he sat on the stool next to him.

"Bartender, fix me two more Incredible Hulks."

Tarron just stared at his drink until the bartender brought him a fresh glass. Slowly, he raised his head and made eye contact with his little brother.

"You want to talk, go ahead. I'm all ears," Tarron slurred.

"I never meant to hurt you, I swear." Jay seemed sincere.

"But you did." Tarron dropped his head in disgust.

"I wanted to tell you. Then, after careful consideration, I figured it was best to allow you your happiness."

"Happy, but living a lie," Tarron said, raising his voice.

"Lie. Truth. Who knows? All I know is that you seemed happy. I wasn't going to be the one to spoil that. My life was already fucked up. You know how embarrassing it was for Mom to find out her bad seed had done it again."

"What do you want from me, Jay?"

"I don't want anything from you. I'm here because of my son," Jay said firmly.

"Who?" Tarron's eyes became enlarged.

"Okay, our son."

"What?"

"Terrance, nigga. Is that what you want me to say? Terrance needs us. I've been watching his behavior, his mannerisms, but most of all, his attitude. I see the anger and the rage building in him, like it did in me. I feel terrible that this situation has come to light, but now we must try to correct it for the better." Jay slammed his glass on the table. "I've been a fuckup all my life. Now I've got a chance to do right by my son!"

"Okay, like I said before, what do you want from me?" Tarron gave Jay the evil eye.

"I need for all of us to see a counselor," Jay said.

"First, the judge sends me to counseling because he thinks me and my no-good better half still want to be together, and now my never-been-shit brother and father of my son believes I need to see another counselor along with a totally dysfunctional family."

"If you won't do it because I want you to, then do it for Terrance. Let's give him every opportunity to settle this hate before it's too late."

"Are you kidding me? I'm the one . . . You know what? It's already too damn late. Jay, just go the fuck on. You put the *l* in *loser*."

Jay slammed his drink down again. "I'm here trying to settle things with you, nigga, and this is the response I get? This spoiled-ass attitude of yours is why you're in this situation now."

"Oh, so now it's my fault you sexed my wife and had the child that should've been my son?" Tarron's stare spelled death. "You better walk now if you know what's good for you, chief." Tarron began to rise from his seat.

"You know what? Screw you, you punk-ass nigga. I knew I shouldn't have come down here. You had things too good all your life. I'm glad I fucked your wife," Jay said, stepping back. He knew those words were meant for fighting.

Before Tarron could get in position, Jay caught him with a right punch that dazed Tarron. He stumbled back into the bar stool. The bartender continued to wipe the excess water from a clean glass.

There was no way Tarron would let his little brother get the best of him. Jay could never beat him. Tarron was too athletic. He grabbed Jay's neck like he was catching a pass thrown by a quarterback. He ran Jay's head right in the end zone. Jay's head met the back wall of the club with force. Once he was down, Tarron extended kicks to Jay's ribs for old and new shit he'd done.

Jay made every attempt to shield himself with his arms, but to no avail. The club bouncers quickly rushed in to protect Jay from Tarron's vicious stomps. As they pulled Tarron from his brother, Jay jumped up as if he was shocked. He stood, blood dripping from his lip.

"I'ma kill you, motherfu . . ." Jay leaped over the shorter bouncer and tackled Tarron to the floor. They fought like two wrestlers on the WWF.

Ray grew tired of watching the commotion and left the VIP lounge. He saw the entire episode unfold on the security cameras in his office. Ray instructed the bouncers to let them both go.

"My son, your nephew, needs us," said Jay as he fixed his shirt. He turned to Tarron before leaving. "I should've filed for custody of Terrance the day Secret met me at the court-house. *Thank her for stopping me!*"

Chapter 26

The next few days were rough for the Jenkins clan. Tarron had many things to contemplate. He knew that if he told Victoria about Secret's e-mails, the family reunion would immediately turn into a disaster. It was already considered borderline psycho, given the fact that Secret had been invited by Motherdear and Tarron's grandmother. The crazier part was that she'd agreed to come.

Secret's e-mails really affected Tarron. He kept thinking about them on the ride down Interstate 95. He tried to get his mind off of Secret by fondling Victoria's leg.

Victoria purposefully moved slightly to let Tarron's hand fall to the side. He glanced over at her, eyebrows raised.

"Victoria, are you going to be straight with everything this weekend?"

"What do you mean?" she asked, turning her attention to the passing cars.

"You know, Secret and the kids will be at the family reunion."

"Whose idea was that?" she asked, with an attitude.

"Motherdear feels like it would be an insult not to invite her after all she's been through. We're the only family she really has."

"Well, Tarron, where does that put me?" Victoria became noticeably irritated.

"Victoria, my family is very loving. They'll understand that you're my woman now."

Victoria rolled her eyes. "I can't tell."

Tarron knew Victoria felt the repercussions from the drama in his life. Not wanting to mess up the mood, he let her comment go. As Tarron pulled up at Granny's house, he gently kissed Victoria on her forehead. "Everything's going to turn out fine. Trust me," he said. Victoria grabbed the door latch and hopped from the car.

Children were playing in the front yard when they walked up. Tarron smiled as he moved Victoria's hand back and forth. He could hear music and more adult voices coming from around the back of the house.

"What kind of barbecue is this?" Victoria asked.

"It's the true old-fashioned, down-home kind. Straight country," Tarron said before being interrupted by Granny Sarah's call.

"Tarron, Tarron, is that you, baby?" shouted a voice from the porch.

"It's me, Granny."

"Where's that pretty wife of yours and my great-grands?"

Tarron turned to make eye contact with Victoria, but the large flap from her purse shielded her from Granny's sight.

"Don't know," Tarron replied.

Victoria closed her purse and gave Granny a large smile, showing a full set of teeth.

"Tarron, who's this pretty little lady you brought witcha?"

"Well, Granny, Secret and I have been separated for some time now. We're going through a complicated divorce. And this is my new girlfriend, Victoria."

"Let me get this straight. You still married to that pretty girl, the mother of your children, and you show up here at the family reunion with another woman. Wow! Times sure have changed. Back in my day, I would have scorched yo ass with a pot of boiling water. So you're a little home wrecker, ha?"

Victoria's face turned beet red. She looked to Tarron for help.

"Oh, don't worry about me. Secret is the one you need to worry about." Granny looked Victoria up and down with cold eyes. She shook her head.

Mortified, Victoria began to shake. She gave Tarron a long stare, as if to say, "Maybe this wasn't a good idea."

"Baby, I'm just kidding with you," said Granny, "but this is some foul mess." She laughed like a country bumpkin.

"Welcome to the family reunion—Jenkins style," Tarron said to Victoria.

"Shit, I thought your grandmother was going to kick my ass," she said.

"Me too!" he replied.

Granny came down off the porch and took Victoria's hand. She led her around back and introduced her to everybody.

"Hey, is that there you, Tarron?" shouted a short man with a scratchy voice.

"You know it's me, Uncle Rosco," Tarron replied.

"Get over here and show me some love, kinfolk."

Tarron walked over and extended his hand, but Uncle Rosco grabbed him close. He began lifting Tarron up and down like a yo-yo.

"Boy, it's good to see you. I see you living

good." Then he released him. "And I see you still know how to pick the ladies. That's one fine little woman you got there. She got a friend or a momma for your Uncle Rosco?"

"I'm not sure, Uncle Rosco."

"If she do, you tell her that my Viagra is on back order. But I'll make a good sugar daddy to somebody when they release my Social Security."

Tarron just shook his head and began walking toward Victoria, who was standing off to the side like a stranger.

"Did I tell you that I'm sorry?" Tarron said.

"Sorry for what?" She seemed distant.

"Sorry for this weekend. If I know my family, something is going to happen. So I'm apologizing now."

"Daddy, Daddy." Screams came from behind Tarron's back.

He turned to see Tika running full speed toward him with open arms. He opened his arms wide, and she jumped in. The impact caused him to stumble back into Victoria. He looked up again and saw Secret and Terrance coming around the corner, holding hands.

"Hello, Tarron," Secret said, ignoring Victoria.

"Hello, Secret."

Tarron put Tika down and held out his hand toward Terrance.

"Give me five, little man."

Terrance looked up at Tarron. He started to give some dap, until his eyes met Victoria's. Then he immediately jetted off.

"What was that all about?" Tarron asked Secret.

"How would I know?" she said, looking Victoria up and down.

"Come on, ladies. Let's go get us some punch." Tarron grabbed Victoria's and Tika's hands, leaving Secret standing alone.

I can't believe he just left me standing here, she thought. *What does she really got that I don't?* Secret stormed toward the gate behind the tree. She tried to be strong and hold back the tears, but they poured from her eyes like a stream.

"Daddy, I want to go play with some of my cousins I haven't seen in a while," Tika said.

"Baby, I haven't seen you in a while. Don't you want to spend some time with me?"

"Mommy said, 'Only say hi to Ms. Victoria, and don't be around her long,' or we both were going to be in big trouble. And Terrance said he hates her, and that he's never coming to visit you anymore as long as she's around." Tika stuck her finger out and pointed straight at Victoria.

"That bitch!" Victoria whispered.

"It's all right, baby. You go play with your cousins," Tarron said.

Victoria crossed her arms over her chest. Her face froze. Tarron knew the words from his daughter's lips had cut Victoria deep. He did not have the words to comfort her. He could only pull her close and hold her tight in his arms. Victoria jerked away.

In her mind, she needed to rethink wanting to be Mrs. Tarron Jenkins. Being involved with a man who already had a ready-made family was starting to take its toll. A slight smile appeared on her face as Jay came out the back door of the house. *Now, there's a Jenkins more my style,* she thought.

"Things are about to get real interesting," Tarron said in Victoria's ear.

"What do you mean?" she asked.

Victoria closely watched Jay as she twirled her finger in her hair. She sipped her lemonade with a strange expression.

"Uh, hello? Is anyone home?" Tarron asked.

"Look, Tarron, don't start. Just let it go," Victoria said.

"Oh, so now you're on his side, too?" Tarron questioned.

Victoria never responded.

Jay moved slowly, never taking his eyes off

of Victoria. He gave her a slight wink as Tarron focused his attention on Uncle Rosco.

"Jay! Is that there you, boy?" asked Uncle Rosco.

"Cool-ass Uncle Rosco," Jay said.

"Yeah, that's me. The smoothest pimp at the Grand Mountain Senior Citizens' Home," he shouted with a hard laugh.

"Come on, Uncle Rosco. You know they revoked your pimp card a long time ago," Jay replied.

"Yeah, they did, but ever since that Viagra, I got it back with an upgrade—double platinum."

Their laughter was drowned out by the other conversations in the backyard, the screaming children running all around, and the music from the speakers that had been placed in the downstairs windows of the house.

Tarron guided Victoria to the double swing in the backyard. Being there would allow him the privacy he needed. He had decided today would be the perfect day to pop the question. Tarron couldn't hold on to the ring any longer.

Before reaching in his pocket, he tugged on Victoria's hand. "Listen, Victoria, I know . . ."

Motherdear slung open the door. "Tarronnn!"

Her timing couldn't be worse, he thought. "Victoria, I'll be back. Let me see what she wants." Tarron searched for her approval.

"I'll be just fine," she replied, with a frown.

Tarron walked into the big house to see what his mother could possibly want. Motherdear was working hard on her mac and tuna salad creation. He used this as a chance to scare her. He crept through the door, making not one sound. "Watch out there now," Tarron yelled, pinching her sides.

He startled his mother something terrible. Motherdear dropped the jar of relish into the bowl she was mixing.

"Damn it, boy, look what the hell you made me do."

"Calm down, old lady. Relish will only help sweeten up the salad. You know all us Jenkins have a sweet tooth, anyhow. You called me. What you want?"

"Boy, you gettin' smart wit me? I just called you 'cause I felt like it," Motherdear said, licking the spoon. "Now, take yo ass back outside," she said, laughing.

"On the real, Mom, I need to talk to you about a few things."

"Got some things on my mind, too." Motherdear put her hands on her hips. "You first," she said.

"I want to hear what you have to say."

"I tried to tell you in those e-mails." Motherdear paused.

Tarron stood in shock. "But, Ma . . . Why? I thought they were from someone who hated me. They were so detailed."

"I know how strongly you feel about your mother putting her two cents into your private affairs. But I felt I had to let you know what was going on." Motherdear looked concerned. "Instead of me actually coming right out and saying it to you, I would give you little hints that would allow you to figure it out for yourself."

"But why didn't you just call me?" he asked. "Jay told me you knew everything, but I didn't believe his lying ass."

"When I went to see your brother in jail, just before you were getting ready to get married, I showed your brother a picture of you and Secret. You know, that Christmas picture you guys gave everybody. As soon as he saw Secret, he bust out laughing, saying, 'I know her. I know her from somewhere.' I asked him where did he know her from, and he told me the whole story."

"Everybody has a different version," Tarron said in disgust. "I don't know who or what to believe."

"When I did the calculations, I realized that

both of you had a fifty-fifty chance of being little Terrance's father." Motherdear stared through the window. "Lord knows, I ain't want no parts of that."

"But your e-mails were so mean. It seemed as if you were teasing me, torturing me to some extent. At first, I thought it was maybe Jay, until I remembered he wasn't smart enough to even send an e-mail. Not even if his life depended on it," Tarron said.

"The e-mails were meant to get your mind racing, the blood flowing, that's all. They were never meant to hurt you. I did it out of love for you, Tarron. You have to understand that," Motherdear replied.

"Do I?"

"Yes. Understand that Secret still loves you, too. Now I'ma get out yo business. But, one more thing before I do. Jay showed me some important paperwork today." Motherdear grabbed Tarron by the hand firmly. "That fool has filed for full custody of Terrance. He says Secret can't handle him anymore, and he's not going to let his son suffer."

Tarron broke away from Motherdear's grip. All her hard work on the tuna casserole now decorated the wall. "This shit is crazy," he yelled. "I'm the only father Terrance has ever known."

Motherdear attempted to console her son

as the door flew open. Several of the kids used the house as a shortcut to get back to their base in the front yard.

"I'm gonna whip all your little butts if you run through this house again," yelled Mother-dear. When she turned back around to finish her talk with Tarron, Uncle Rosco came walking into the house.

"Did somebody die?" he asked. "And what the hell is the tuna casserole doing on the wall?"

"Everything is great, you old fool," Mother-dear responded.

"Come on, Tarron. I need me a Spades partner," said Uncle Rosco.

"I'm talking with my mother right now," he replied.

"Go on. We can finish this talk later. Go and enjoy yourself," she responded as she began to wipe the casserole from the wall.

Tarron walked outside with Uncle Rosco. Instead of following him to the table, he asked his cousin Marcus to take his spot. Tarron spotted Victoria and remembered the proposal. He pulled the ring from his pocket and headed her way.

"Excuse me, miss. Is this seat taken?"

She gave him a three-dollar smile. "I'm saving this seat for my man," Victoria said. "Tarron, we need to talk."

"But wait. Me first," he said.

Before she could respond, Secret stood over top of them with her hands on her hips.

"Not now," he said in a hostile tone.

"Now!" Secret responded.

Tarron kissed Victoria on her forehead and stood up to talk to Secret. Secret told him to follow her, because everyone didn't need to be in their conversation. She looked directly at Victoria. As Tarron walked away, Victoria watched them both as they disappeared. Tarron couldn't believe he'd left Victoria only to read a letter Secret shoved in his face.

Everyone is guilty at one time or another of taking people in life for granted. I was no exception, until my eyes were opened wide. I often think about all the good times we had. And to think this moment might be our last.

It wasn't an accident that made me lose you, but another woman that stole you. But I know that she could never love you like I do.

I've been there for you from the start. We've built our lives together. And, now you want to throw it all away.

I know she says that she loves you, but besides those words, what else does she do to prove her love? She hasn't been through any rough times with you. How do you know that she really loves you? Just think, she messes

*with married men. If she does it with you,
she'll do it to you. It hurts me to see her toy
with your heart in this way. She could never
love you like I do.*

Both women in his triangle were now out of
sight. Tarron sat confused, but glad that
Secret had stepped away. Suddenly, he had
several flashbacks. His mind rotated from the
delivery room, where he held Secret's hand
for the birth of Terrance, to looking down the
aisle as Secret walked toward him at their wedding. Moments later he opened his eyes to
find Victoria bent up in the chair at the hospital. He needed counseling *bad*.

Tarron was losing his mind. He balled the
letter up and concealed it in his pocket, next
to the ring. As he jetted back to Victoria's
side, he could tell she was frustrated. Instantly,
he saw Jay from the corner of his eye, leaving
the swing area.

"Did he say something to you?" Tarron
asked as he approached Victoria.

She stood. "Tarron, I'm tired now. I
thought I would just call it an evening. I'm
going upstairs to sleep."

"But it's only six o'clock."

"But I'm tired," she responded in a nasty
tone.

"I'll be up in a minute. I put the bags in our room," he said.

"No need to rush. This is your family re-union, and you shouldn't miss any of the fun just to lie with me."

As Victoria walked away, Motherdear sat next to her son. "You have a good woman and the mother of your children over there. It is wrong for you to punish her when your record isn't squeaky clean."

Tarron stared straight ahead.

"What you need to do is to go over there and fix your family. The only ones in the long run to be really hurt are those children. Re-member your upbringing and do the right thing."

Tarron left Motherdear and found Secret talking with some of his family members.

"Can we talk?" Tarron asked.

The two walked down the old path beyond the back of the house. Tarron took the time to discuss how hurt he was because of Ter-rance. The way he expressed himself made Secret feel good. It was the first time in months that they'd realized their mistakes.

Secret expressed her love for him over and over again. After hours of trying to reconcile, they embraced. She told him that because of a reservation glitch at the hotel, Motherdear had insisted that she stay in one of the bedrooms upstairs.

"I'll leave my door unlocked," she said. "When you come to your senses, just come home." Secret spoke with conviction. "This offer is only good for tonight," she said, staring Tarron in the eye.

As Secret called for the kids, Tarron noticed the weirdness in Secret's voice. Tarron couldn't put his finger on it, but something wasn't right. However, it was getting late, and he wanted to say good night to his children.

The house was full of people drinking and telling childhood stories. Secret was the first adult other than Victoria to call it a night. When Secret strolled past Tarron, she reminded him of the open-door policy.

Tarron sat in the living room in deep thought. *Do I throw away years of marriage over one mistake? Will Victoria love me in good times and bad? Is she worth it? Hell, will I want Victoria after I'm married to her? If I stay with Secret, how will I ever stomach seeing Jay and Secret near each other?*

His head pounded like a beating drum. He was in a losing situation. However, he'd reached a decision. This decision would make one happy and the other sad.

Tarron climbed the stairs. Each step echoed

in his head. As he reached the middle of the hallway and stood between the bedroom doors, to one side was his wife, the mother of his children. On the other was his lifetime soul mate, who made him feel complete.

Tarron reached for the doorknob, twisted it, and slowly entered the room.

The next morning everyone woke up to the screams coming from the hallway. Startled by Terrance's and Tika's echoing cries, Tarron came crashing from his room to see what had happened. His heart dropped as he watched Tika squirm down the wall, falling flat on the floor.

"My word," said Motherdear. "Can't nobody get some sleep around here!" She came from her room, tying her robe. "Oh, my Lord," she said, running for Tika.

"Mom, what is going on?" Tarron yelled as he and Motherdear met up at the same time. They stood outside the room where Secret slept. The door was wide open.

Victoria stood in her doorway, wondering what was going on. She was glad that Tarron had finally left her side. Victoria had come to some final decisions of her own.

Tika clenched her father's leg, pointing in the direction of her mother's room. Tarron glanced in and saw blood all over the sheets. His jaw dropped.

"Oh no," Uncle Rosco screamed. "Get in there! Somebody call the ambulance!"

"Move back," Jay said, rushing past Tarron, who still stood in shock. "Why is everybody standing around? Get some towels!"

Uncle Rosco moved with as much speed as he possibly could. Tarron and Jay rushed to Secret's side. Although Terrance remained locked on his mother, he reached for the phone, pressing 911.

"What in God's name is going on in there?" Motherdear asked. She sat in the hall, holding Tika.

No one answered.

Tarron tried to pull Terrance and loosen the grip he held on his mom.

Terrance screamed, "No, get off of me! Wake up, Mom."

"Come on, son. The ambulance will be here shortly." Jay picked up the razor from the floor. Both wrists were slit! Jay made eye contact with Tarron, realizing she was already dead.

Terrance behaved like a stubborn mule. Nothing could make him move. His clothes were drenched in Secret's blood, and his expression showed that he knew she was gone.

As the paramedics jetted into the room,

Terrance finally moved. After minutes of observation, Secret was ready to be covered with the white sheet. Motherdear held her composure as she escorted everyone from the room. Tarron looked back one last time as he wiped the blood from his hand.

An hour passed before the body was taken out. The mood was somber when Tarron began to speak. "I don't know what else can happen." He stood to his feet and grabbed for Victoria. On the verge of breaking down, he reached to embrace her. Her cold response upset him even more.

"I can't stay here any longer. Mom, we're leaving." He looked at the children. "Can you watch them for a few days, until I can make the funeral arrangements?"

"Of course," Motherdear answered.

"Don't go, Daddy," Tika cried.

"Don't worry. I'll be back to get you." He squatted to touch her face. "I have to take care of a few things . . . you know, get myself together. Besides, way too much has happened—from *secrets* to now *death*." Tarron stood and turned to Victoria for comfort.

"Tarron, there's just one more secret," Victoria said.

In a daze, he stood.

"Do you hear me?"

Jay moved closer to his brother. He placed

his arm around his shoulder as Victoria spoke before him.

"I said, I have one more secret."

"What is it? I don't think my heart can handle any more."

"I'm leaving with Jay. And we're going to fight for custody of Terrance."

Jay stared straight into Victoria's eyes. He was speechless. A large smile came across his face. He reached over to kiss Victoria. *Love sure does work in mysterious ways,* he thought.

To be continued . . .

About the Author

J. Tremble is a product of the Washington, D.C., public school system. He graduated from Woodrow Wilson High School. He received his BA in psychology in 1993 from Missouri Valley College and his master's in elementary education from Howard University in 1999.

J. Tremble has worked the past eight years as a sixth-grade math teacher in the Prince George's County public school system. He is a first-time author and is currently working on his second novel. J. Tremble has written several children's and poetry books.

He is a loving father, devoted husband, and active participant in his community. J. Tremble works with foster care boys in an independent-living program. He coaches in the Boys and Girls Club and coordinates an after-school step program at his middle school. J. Tremble is a member of Phi Beta Sigma Fraternity, Incorporated.

GREAT BOOKS,
GREAT SAVINGS!

When You Visit Our Website:
www.kensingtonbooks.com
You Can Save Money Off The Retail Price
Of Any Book You Purchase!

- **All Your Favorite Kensington Authors**
- **New Releases & Timeless Classics**
- **Overnight Shipping Available**
- **eBooks Available For Many Titles**
- **All Major Credit Cards Accepted**

Visit Us Today To Start Saving!
www.kensingtonbooks.com

All Orders Are Subject To Availability.
Shipping and Handling Charges Apply.
Offers and Prices Subject To Change Without Notice.

Look For These Other
Dafina Novels

If I Could
0-7582-0131-1

by Donna Hill
  $6.99US/**$9.99**CAN

Thunderland
0-7582-0247-4

by Brandon Massey
  $6.99US/**$9.99**CAN

June In Winter
0-7582-0375-6

by Pat Phillips
  $6.99US/**$9.99**CAN

Yo Yo Love
0-7582-0239-3

by Daaimah S. Poole
  $6.99US/**$9.99**CAN

When Twilight Comes
0-7582-0033-1

by Gwynne Forster
  $6.99US/**$9.99**CAN

It's A Thin Line
0-7582-0354-3

by Kimberla Lawson Roby
  $6.99US/**$9.99**CAN

Perfect Timing
0-7582-0029-3

by Brenda Jackson
  $6.99US/**$9.99**CAN

Never Again Once More
0-7582-0021-8

by Mary B. Morrison
  $6.99US/**$8.99**CAN

Available Wherever Books Are Sold!

Check out our website at www.kensingtonbooks.com.